W9-BXG-769

The Adventures of Pinocchio

The Adventures of Pinocchio

BY CARLO COLLODI
Retold by Neil Morris

ILLUSTRATED BY FRANK BABER

RAND McNALLY & COMPANY
Chicago · New York · San Francisco

Contents

Published in the U.S.A. in 1982
by Rand McNally and Company

Library of Congress Catalog Card Number: 82-60188
Printed in Spain by Graficas Reunidas, S.A., Madrid

Introduction

The story of Pinocchio, a wooden puppet who longs to become a real boy, is a hundred years old. Its author was an Italian writer named Carlo Lorenzini who took his pen-name, Collodi, from the name of the village where he was born. The village of Collodi, some 36 miles from Florence, is now famous and has a permanent exhibition garden dedicated to the adventures of Pinocchio.

First published as a children's magazine serial in 1881, Pinocchio's adventures were collected into a book in 1883. Since then they have never ceased to be popular and the name of the likeable rascal whose happy-go-lucky approach to life leads him from one disaster to the next, has become world famous. The book has been translated from Italian into over 80 languages, made into films and television series, been the subject of academic theses—and been loved by generations of children.

For this new edition, the text has been retold in modern English. Following faithfully the original story and retaining all the original characters, it brings Pinocchio's world, a wonderful mixture of magical situations and real human characteristics, back to life.

The artist

Frank Baber was born in Lancashire, England and received his training at Bolton College of Art. He has spent all his working life (apart from war service) as a practising artist, working in such varied fields as advertising illustration, textile design, the theatre, architecture, portrait painting and book illustration. His pictures have been exhibited by the Royal Society of Portrait Painters, the Royal Society of British Artists and the Manchester Academy. He has four children and five grandchildren.

The piece of wood

Once upon a time there was a piece of wood. It looked just like a very ordinary piece of wood, the kind you throw on the fire to make a good blaze and warm the room up. Most people would not have given it a second glance. However, one day this ordinary piece of wood found itself lying on the floor of a carpenter's workshop in Italy and there its strange adventures began.

The carpenter's name was Master Antonio but everyone called him Master Cherry because the tip of his nose was as red and as shiny as a ripe, red cherry. Master Cherry made wonderful tables, chairs and cupboards. He was just looking for something to use as the leg of a small table when he noticed the very ordinary piece of wood lying on the floor at his feet.

"You have come at just the right time," he said and, deciding to set to work on it at once, he picked up a sharp axe to remove the rough bark, twigs and knot-holes.

To his surprise, when he raised the axe, he heard a small voice say: "Please do not cut me!" The carpenter looked all round the workshop but there was no-one there. He looked under the bench, in the tool cupboard, he even looked in the basket of shavings and sawdust, but he found nothing. Then he laughed to himself. "All in my imagination," he said and, picking up the axe, he struck a tremendous blow on the piece of wood.

"Oh! Ouch! That hurt!" cried the same small voice. This time Master Cherry was really alarmed. He stood there with his mouth

open, staring at the piece of wood. Where on earth could the voice be coming from? Surely not from the wood?

"Perhaps there is someone hidden inside it," said the carpenter. "We'll soon see about that." And he grabbed the piece of wood and began to hit it against the wall.

Then he stopped and listened carefully. He waited for two minutes—nothing; five minutes—nothing; ten minutes—still nothing.

"All in my imagination," he said again, forcing himself to laugh. Putting down the axe, he picked up his plane and started to run it up and down the piece of wood. As he did so, the small voice started giggling: "Oh, do stop. That tickles!"

This time poor Master Cherry was sure there must be a ghost in his workshop and he fainted right away. When at last he opened his eyes, he found himself sitting on the floor. His face was quite white and the tip of his nose, instead of being red and shiny, was blue with fright.

At that moment someone knocked at the door. It was Geppetto, a man who was known to the children of the district as Polendina (which means corn pudding) because he wore a yellow wig which looked just like a cornmeal pudding. In those days it was usual for both men and women to wear wigs and white ones were fashionable. Poor Geppetto's cheap white wig had turned yellow with age and the name Polendina reminded him how shabby he looked and made him fly into a rage whenever he heard it.

"Good day, Master Antonio," he said. "What are you doing there on the floor?"

"Teaching the ants the alphabet," said Master Cherry crossly. "Now what can I do for you?"

"This morning I had an idea," said Geppetto. "I thought I would make a wooden puppet, a wonderful puppet that could dance, fence and jump like an acrobat. And with this puppet I could travel the world and earn my living. What do you think?"

"Bravo, Polendina!" cried a small voice.

Hearing himself called Polendina, Geppetto went red in the face and turned on the carpenter. "Why do you insult me?" he shouted, grabbing Master Cherry and pulling him to his feet.

"I didn't say a word," said the carpenter weakly.

"Yes, you did!"

"No, I didn't!"

"Yes, you did!"

"No, I didn't!"

Very soon they came to blows and fought so fiercely that in the end they each pulled off the other's wig. This gave them both such a shock that they stopped fighting and, handing back the wigs, shook hands and decided to make friends. Geppetto replaced his wig.

"You still haven't told me what I can do for you," said Master Cherry.

"I need some wood to make my puppet. Will you give me some?"

Master Cherry was delighted to have the chance to get rid of the piece of wood that had caused him such a fright. He picked up the wood cautiously but, just as he was about to hand it over, it wriggled from his hands and struck Geppetto hard on the shins.

"So that's the way you give your presents!" cried Geppetto.

"No it wasn't me, it was the wood . . . " said Master Cherry.

"I know it was the wood. But it was you that hit me with it!"

"No, it wasn't!"

"Yes, it was!"

"No, it wasn't, Polendina!"

"Ass!"

"Polendina!"

"Donkey!"

"Polendina!"

On hearing himself called Polendina for the third time, Geppetto went even redder in the face and he grabbed the carpenter again. This time Master Cherry ended up with two scratches on his nose and Geppetto had two buttons torn from his waistcoat. Then at last they were satisfied, agreed to call it a draw and swore to be friends for the rest of their lives.

Geppetto took the piece of wood and, thanking Master Cherry, limped off to his own house to start work on his puppet.

Pinocchio runs away

Geppetto was very poor and he lived in a small, two-roomed house with very simple furniture. Apart from his carpenter's tools he only had a chair and a broken-down old table downstairs. At the end of the room there was a fireplace with a painted fire and by the fire a painted saucepan was boiling away cheerfully. Geppetto thought this was better than nothing, as he could not afford the real thing.

As soon as he reached home, Geppetto took out his tools and started to make the puppet. "I think I shall call him Pinocchio," he said to himself as he worked. "That name will bring him luck." Having decided on a name, he started to work faster. First he made the hair, then the forehead and then the eyes.

When he had finished the eyes, Geppetto noticed with astonishment that they moved from side to side and then looked straight at him. "Why are you looking at me like that, wooden eyes?" he asked, but there was no reply.

Next he carved the nose. No sooner had he made it than it began to grow. The nose just grew and grew, so Geppetto started cutting it off. To his surprise, the more he cut it, the longer the nose became! In the end he managed to carve a funny, cheeky-looking nose that turned up at the end. With that he had to be satisfied. Next he started work on the mouth, but he had not even finished when it started to laugh at him.

"Stop it!" shouted Geppetto. "Stop laughing at once!" The mouth stopped laughing, but poked out its tongue as far as it would go.

Geppetto pretended not to notice this and went on working. He made the chin next, then the neck, the shoulders, the body, and then the arms and hands. He had hardly finished the hands when they snatched his wig from his head and before Geppetto could do anything, the puppet had put the yellow wig on himself.

Geppetto looked sad. "Pinocchio, you naughty boy," he said. "You are not even finished and already you are cheeky to your father. Now behave yourself!" Hoping that this would impress the puppet, he worked on and made the legs and feet. As soon as they were finished, the feet gave him a kick in the face.

"It's my own fault," Geppetto said to himself. "I should have known he would do something like that." Then he took the puppet and put him on the floor. Leading him by the hand, he showed Pinocchio how to walk and, after a while, the puppet's stiff legs started to move on their own. At first he walked unsteadily, then he ran around the room and finally he ran out of the door into the street.

Geppetto ran after him, but Pinocchio was too fast and clattered off down the street. "Stop! Stop him!" cried Geppetto, but when the people in the street saw a wooden puppet running so fast, they just stood and watched in astonishment.

As luck would have it, a soldier came round the corner at that moment and, hearing the uproar, he stood in the middle of the road and waited for the little figure to reach him. Pinocchio tried to slip through his legs, but the soldier caught hold of him by the nose and carried him to Geppetto, who came panting up behind.

Geppetto was very angry with the puppet and looked at him sternly. Then he took him by the arm and led him away. "I'll teach you a thing or two when we get home," Geppetto said roughly. At this Pinocchio threw himself on the ground and refused to take another step. "Don't beat me, please!" he pleaded, pretending to cry. People began to crowd around

and many of them felt sorry for Pinocchio. "Poor little puppet," they said. "He will get a terrible hiding when he gets home. Geppetto must be a real bully. He will beat that poor little puppet to pieces!"

Pinocchio sobbed and pleaded and the crowd muttered, until at last the soldier picked Pinocchio up, told him to run along and led Geppetto off to prison. Geppetto sobbed all the way. "Naughty boy!" he said. "And to think how hard I worked to make him. But it's my own fault. I should have known he would be like that."

As poor Geppetto was being led away, Pinocchio ran off as fast as he could. He was soon out in the fields and before long he was jumping over hedges and leaping across ditches like a racehorse.

When he started to feel tired, he found his way back to the town and went to Geppetto's house. He pushed open the door, went in and lay down on the floor. He heaved a big sigh of satisfaction and settled down to sleep.

He did not rest for long, however, for after a few minutes he heard a strange noise, like a ghostly voice: "Cri-cri-cri." Pinocchio was frightened. "Who's there?" he called.

"It's only me." Pinocchio turned round and saw a big cricket crawling up the wall.

"Who are you?" asked Pinocchio.

"I am the talking cricket, and I have lived in this room for more than a hundred years."

"Well now this room is mine," said the puppet, "so you'd better get out at once!"

"I will not go," replied the cricket, "until I have told you a great truth."

"Tell it then, but be quick about it!" snapped Pinocchio.

"Woe betide children who disobey their parents or run away from home," said the cricket slowly. "Sooner or later they will regret it and come to a bad end."

"You can preach as much as you like," said Pinocchio. "As for me, I have made up my mind to run away at dawn tomorrow. Otherwise I shall be sent to school like the other children and forced to learn and work. But I don't want to learn. It is much more fun chasing butterflies, climbing trees or spending the day fishing and swimming in the river."

"You poor thing!" said the cricket. "Don't you know that if you don't learn anything you'll grow up to be an ass and everyone will make fun of you?"

"Be quiet!" shouted Pinocchio, but the cricket went on patiently, "If you don't want to go to school, at least learn a trade so that you can earn an honest living."

"There is only one trade that I fancy," replied Pinocchio, "and that is to eat, drink, sleep and enjoy myself, lazing about from morning to night."

"People in that trade usually end up in hospital or in prison!" said the cricket calmly. "Poor Pinocchio! I really pity you! After all, you are only a puppet and, worst of all, you have a wooden head."

At these words Pinocchio jumped up in a rage and, snatching a hammer from the bench, threw it at the cricket. Perhaps he didn't really mean to hurt him, but unfortunately it was a direct hit and the poor cricket fell straight down from the wall and lay quite still.

Pinocchio is hungry

It was starting to grow dark and, realizing that he had not eaten all day, Pinocchio began to feel hungry. It was not long before the feeling of hunger became unbearable. Pinocchio thought he was starving to death!

He quickly ran to the fireplace where he saw the saucepan boiling away and reached out to take off the lid. Only then did he realize that the fire and the saucepan were not real at all, but only painted on the wall. The tip of his turned-up nose drooped with disappointment—and his stomach felt emptier than ever.

He rushed round the room, searching in every corner for food. If only he could find an old crust of bread or a dog's bone—anything to chew on. But there was nothing at all. As his hunger grew worse, Pinocchio started to splutter and yawn; his yawns were so big that his mouth almost reached his ears.

At last he began to cry desperately: "The

cricket was right. I was wrong to disobey my father and to run away from home. If father were here now he would help me. Oh what a terrible thing it is to starve!"

Just then he saw something round and white in a pile of dust. Snatching it up, he was delighted to find that it was an egg. At first he thought it must be a dream, and he turned the egg over in his wooden hands, feeling it and then kissing it.

"Now how shall I cook it?" he asked himself. "Shall I make an omelette, or fry it, or simply boil it? No, the quickest way is just to cook it in a saucer. Oh, I'm so hungry! I hope I don't faint before it's ready."

Pinocchio searched round for a few coals and wood-shavings, put them in a heap in the fireplace and made a real fire. When it was hot enough, he put some water in a saucer and placed it on the coals. Then he cracked the egg-shell over the saucer. Instead of the egg white and yolk he was hoping for, out popped a little chick!

"Thank you, master Pinocchio," cheeped the chick. "You have saved me the trouble of breaking my shell. Until we meet again, farewell!" With this the chick hopped onto the table and fluttered out of the window.

Poor Pinocchio just stood there with the egg-shell in his hand. Then he began to cry and scream, stamping his feet on the floor and sobbing, "Oh, the cricket was right. If I had not run away from home and if father were here now, I would not be dying of hunger. Oh, what a terrible thing it is to starve!"

As he now felt hungrier than ever, Pinocchio decided the only thing to do was to leave the house and go off in search of food.

It was a stormy night, full of loud claps of thunder and flashes of lightning. Pinocchio was frightened of the thunder, but his hunger was stronger than his fear so he braved the storm and set out for the centre of the town, running all the way.

The streets of the town were dark and deserted. The shops were closed and there was nobody about. In his despair Pinocchio looked for the nearest doorbell and rang it again and again. A little old man put his head out of the upstairs window. "What do you want at this hour?" he called.

"Please would you be kind enough to spare me a crust of bread?" asked Pinocchio politely.

"Wait there, I'll be back in a minute," said the little old man, thinking that this must be one of those naughty boys who ring people's bells at night to disturb them. When he came back, the old man shouted down: "Come and stand beneath the window."

Pinocchio did as he was told, but as soon as he was under the window the old man poured a whole bucket of cold water over him, soaking him from head to toe. He went off home like a wet dog, tired and still very hungry. As soon as he was back inside the house, he bolted the door and sat down by the fireplace, resting his wet feet on the heap of hot coals to dry. Then in spite of his hunger, he fell fast asleep.

While Pinocchio slept, the heap of coals smouldered and glowed and his wooden feet caught fire and gradually burned away. Pinocchio was so fast asleep that he did not even notice, but went on snoring, as if his feet belonged to someone else. At daybreak he was woken by a knock at the door. "Who's there?" he asked, yawning and rubbing his eyes.

"It's me," said a loud voice. The voice was Geppetto's. He had returned.

Pinocchio's new clothes

Poor Pinocchio had not yet realized that his wooden feet had burned away. When he heard Geppetto's voice, he slipped off his stool to go and open the door. At first he stumbled, then he fell flat on his face.

"Open this door!" cried Geppetto.

"Father, I can't," answered the puppet, rolling around on the floor helplessly.

"Why can't you?"

"Because my feet have been eaten."

"And who has eaten your feet?"

"The cat!" said Pinocchio, seeing that there was a cat asleep in the corner of the room. "I can't stand up, please believe me. Poor me, I shall have to walk on my knees for the rest of my life!"

Thinking that the puppet was playing another of his tricks, Geppetto flew into a rage. First he tried to break the door down, but it was too firmly bolted. At last he managed to climb in through the window. He started to shout angrily at Pinocchio but he saw at once that this time Pinocchio was telling the truth. He really had lost his feet. Geppetto knelt down and took

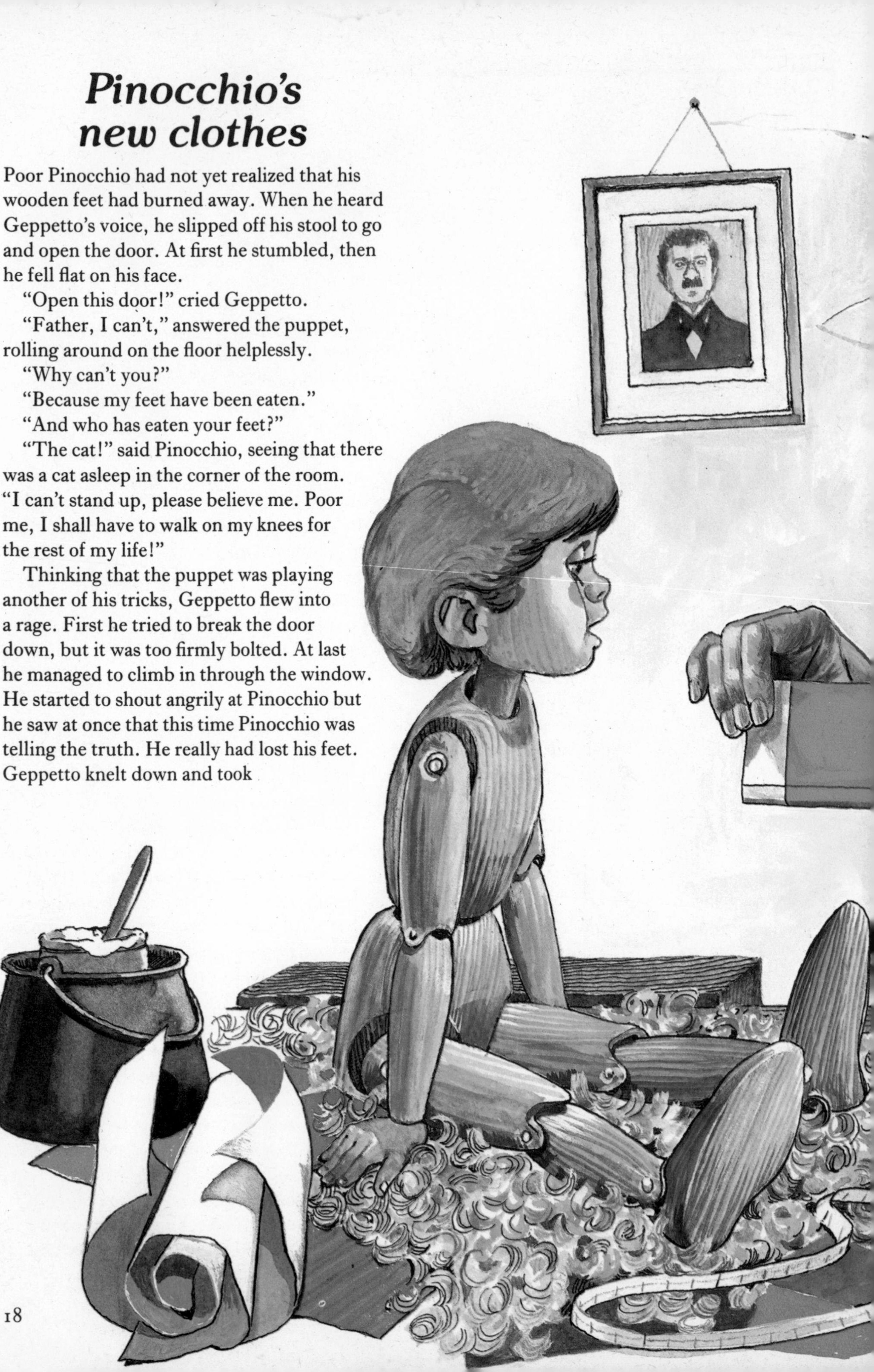

Pinocchio in his arms to comfort him and, with tears rolling down his cheeks, he asked: "How did my poor little Pinocchio manage to burn his feet?"

"I don't know, father," replied Pinocchio, "but I have had a terrible night. There was thunder and lightning and I was very hungry and then the cricket said it served me right and I was only a puppet with a wooden head and I threw a hammer at him, but it was his fault because I didn't mean to kill him, and then I cracked an egg and a chick jumped out and thanked me and said farewell and I got even hungrier, so a little old man told me to stand under his window and he poured a bucket of water over me, but asking for a crust of bread isn't wrong, is it? And I came home and put my feet on the coals to dry and then you knocked on the door and I found my feet had been burned off and I'm still hungry and I haven't got any feet any more . . . " With this Pinocchio burst into tears.

All that Geppetto had really understood from Pinocchio's long tale was that he was dying of hunger, so at once he pulled three pears from his pocket. "I was going to have these for my breakfast," he said, "but you have them, they will do you good."

"If you expect me to eat those, you'd better peel them first," replied Pinocchio.

Geppetto was astonished. "Peel them? You'd better not be so fussy, my boy. In this world you have to eat everything you are offered and be grateful for what you get, for there's no telling where your next meal may come from."

"I expect you're right," said Pinocchio, "but I never eat fruit that hasn't been peeled. I can't stand skin."

So Geppetto fetched a knife and peeled the three pears, putting the skin on the table. Having eaten the first pear in a couple of mouthfuls, Pinocchio was about to throw away the core, but Geppetto caught hold of his arm and stopped him.

"I am certainly not going to eat the core!" shouted the puppet.

Geppetto said nothing but kept the three cores and put them on the table with the skin. When he had scoffed all the pears, Pinocchio said: "I'm still hungry! Don't you have anything else for me to eat?"

"Only the skin and the cores," replied Geppetto.

"Oh well," sighed Pinocchio, "I suppose that's better than nothing." And with a screwed-up face he ate the pear skin and the cores. When there was nothing left at all, he said happily, "Now I feel better."

"So you see," said Geppetto quietly, "I was right when I said you had better not be so fussy. You never know what may happen to you in this world or what you may have to eat. There's no telling!"

Now that he was no longer hungry, Pinocchio began to cry and grumble because he wanted a new pair of feet. "Why should I make you new feet?" asked Geppetto. "So that you can run away from me again, perhaps?"

Pinocchio promised that from now on he would be good. "And I promise that I will go to school and work hard," he said.

"Children always say that when they want something," replied Geppetto.

"But I'm not like other children," insisted Pinocchio. "I always tell the truth, and I promise that I will learn a trade so that I can look after you in your old age."

When he heard this, Geppetto's eyes filled with tears and he went to get his tools and two small pieces of wood. In less than an hour the feet were finished and Geppetto told Pinocchio to shut his eyes and go to sleep. After a while Pinocchio pretended to be asleep and Geppetto gently glued his new feet in place. He did it so carefully and well that you could not even see the join. When Geppetto had finished, Pinocchio opened his eyes, jumped down from the table and began to run around the room.

"To show you how grateful I am," he said, "I shall go to school at once. But first I need some clothes."

So Geppetto made him a shirt out of paper, a pair of shoes from the bark of a tree and a cap out of cardboard. Pinocchio put them on and was very pleased with the way he looked; but he was still not completely happy. "There is still something else I need for school," he said. "I must have an alphabet book. We can go to the shop and buy one."

"But I haven't a single penny," replied Geppetto sadly. This made Pinocchio very sad too and, seeing this, Geppetto suddenly put on his old overcoat and rushed out of the house.

When he returned, Geppetto was no longer wearing his coat although it was cold and wet outside. In his hand was a brand-new alphabet book.

"Where is your coat, father?" asked Pinocchio.

"I sold it," replied Geppetto.

"But why did you sell it?"

"Because I was too hot in it," came the reply.

Pinocchio knew very well why his father had sold the coat. Without saying anything, he jumped up, threw his arms round Geppetto and gave him a great big kiss.

At the puppet theatre

As soon as it stopped raining Pinocchio set off for school with the alphabet book under his arm. On his way he began to think a thousand thoughts. "Today at school I shall learn to read at once, then tomorrow I shall write, and then next day I'll count. After that I shall earn a lot of money and can buy father a beautiful new cloth coat. But what am I thinking? The coat will not be made of cloth, but of gold and silver with diamond buttons. Poor father deserves it after selling his own coat to buy me a book, and in this cold, too."

As he went along, Pinocchio thought he could hear the sounds of pipes and drums. He stopped to listen. The sounds were coming from a street that led to a part of the town he did not know. Pinocchio wanted to find out who was playing the music, but he knew that he was supposed to go to school.

"I know," he said to himself, "today I shall go and listen to the music and tomorrow I shall go to school." And with this he ran off in the direction from which the sounds were coming.

After a few minutes he found himself in a square full of people. They were all crowding round a colourful building made of wood and canvas.

"What is that building?" Pinocchio asked a boy standing next to him.

"Why don't you read the sign?" replied the boy.

"I would read it," said Pinocchio quickly, "but it so happens that I can't read today."

The boy laughed and told Pinocchio that the sign read "Teatro", the Italian word for theatre. He explained that a puppet show was about to begin, and that it cost twopence to get in. Pinocchio was so curious and excited that he asked the boy: "Will you lend me twopence till tomorrow?"

"I would," said the boy in a voice just like Pinocchio's, "but it so happens that I can't lend twopence today."

"I'll sell you my shirt for twopence," said the puppet, jumping up and down with anxiety.

TEATRO

CAFFE
FUOCH
ARTISS

"What use is that?" replied the boy. "A paper shirt's no good in the rain!"

"Will you buy my shoes then?"

"They're no use except for lighting the fire!"

"Well what about my cap?"

"That would only do for feeding mice!"

Pinocchio was in a terrible state by now, and he knew he would do anything to get twopence. He took a deep breath and asked, "Will you give me twopence for this brand-new alphabet book?"

"I don't buy things from other children," replied the boy, who had much more sense than Pinocchio. And he ran off.

"I'll buy it!" said a voice suddenly. It was a seller of old clothes, who had been listening to the conversation. So Pinocchio sold him the book for twopence, without a thought for poor old Geppetto, who was trembling with cold in his shirt sleeves so that his son could have an alphabet book.

Pinocchio paid his twopence and went into the puppet theatre. The curtain was already up and the play had begun. On the stage Harlequin and Mr. Punch were arguing, as they always do, and the audience was screaming with laughter.

All of a sudden Harlequin stopped arguing and, turning to the audience, pointed and said dramatically: "Good heavens! Am I dreaming? Surely that's Pinocchio!"

"It *is* Pinocchio!" cried Mr. Punch. "It is indeed!" added Miss Rose, peeping from behind the curtain. Before long all the puppets joined in the shouting and they all jumped onto the stage. "Good old Pinocchio," shouted Harlequin. "Come up here and say hello to all your wooden brothers and sisters!" Pinocchio jumped over seats and stepped on people's heads to get onto the stage as quickly as he could. Once he was there, all the puppets threw their arms round him and greeted him in the most friendly way. This went on for some time and the audience became impatient and started to shout for the play to continue. The puppets were so excited that they took no notice. They were too busy with Pinocchio.

They were just lifting him onto their shoulders for a triumphal ride when the puppet master appeared. He was very big and so ugly that he would have frightened anyone. His black beard was so long that it touched the ground and he carried a whip made of snakes' and foxes' tails twisted together, which he cracked constantly. When he appeared there was a deathly silence.

The puppet master turned to Pinocchio. "Why are you making all this noise in my theatre?" he asked in a loud, gruff voice.

"Believe me, sir, it was not my fault," replied Pinocchio.

"That's enough!" shouted the puppet master. "We shall sort this matter out tonight. Get on with the play!"

When the play was over, the puppet master went off to the kitchen for his supper. A whole sheep was roasting on a spit, but there was not enough wood on the fire to finish browning the meat. The puppet master called Harlequin and Mr. Punch.

"Bring that new puppet here," he growled. "He is made of very dry wood and will make an excellent blaze."

Harlequin and Mr. Punch hesitated, but when they saw the terrible look on the puppet master's face they ran off. After a short while they returned carrying Pinocchio, who was struggling desperately and screaming: "Father! Father! Save me!"

The puppet master's name was Fire-eater, and although he looked very frightening, he was not a bad man at heart. When he saw poor Pinocchio struggling and screaming, he felt sorry for him and gave a loud sneeze. At this Harlequin began to smile and whispered to Pinocchio, "It's good that the master has sneezed, brother. That means that he has taken pity on you. He always sneezes when he feels sorry for someone!"

"Stop your crying!" the puppet master shouted at Pinocchio. "You are giving me a stomach-ache . . . I feel . . . Atishoo! Atishoo!" He sneezed again twice.

"Bless you!" said Pinocchio.

"Thank you," said Fire-eater. "What about your father and mother, are they still alive?"

"My father is," replied Pinocchio. "I have never known my mother."

"How sad your father would be to see you on the fire," said the puppet master. "Poor old man. Atishoo! Atishoo! Atishoo!"

"Bless you!" said Pinocchio politely.

"Thank you. Still, I must find some wood somewhere, otherwise my meat will not be properly roasted. I have taken pity on you, so instead I shall have to burn one of the other puppets." At this he called over two wooden soldiers.

Fire-eater spoke to them gruffly. "Take Harlequin, tie him up, and then throw him on the fire. I like my meat well roasted."

Poor Harlequin was so terrified that his legs gave way and he fell flat on his face. When Pinocchio saw this, he threw himself at the puppet master's feet and said in a pleading voice: "Have mercy, Sir Fire-eater!"

"There are no sirs here," said Fire-eater.

"Have mercy, Sir Knight!"

"There are no knights here."

"Have mercy, Commander!"

"There are no Commanders here."

"Have mercy, Your Excellency!"

On hearing this the puppet master began to smile. "I beg of you to have mercy on poor Harlequin," said Pinocchio quickly.

"But I must have some wood to put on the fire," replied the puppet master, "for I must have my meat well roasted."

"In that case," said Pinocchio, standing up straight, "I must do my duty. Come here, soldiers, and tie me up. It is not fair that my friend Harlequin should die in my place."

When they heard these brave words, all the puppets, including the two soldiers, began to cry. At first Fire-eater remained unmoved but after a while he started to sneeze again. Then he opened his arms and said to Pinocchio, "You are a good, brave boy. Come here to me!" Pinocchio jumped into his arms and gave him a big kiss on the nose.

"Am I saved?" asked poor Harlequin.

"You are saved," replied Fire-eater. "Tonight I shall have to eat my meat half raw, but it won't happen again, I promise you!"

Hearing this, the puppets all ran back to the stage and began to jump and dance about happily. And they went on dancing all night.

The fox and the cat

Next day Fire-eater took Pinocchio to one side and asked him what his father's name was.

"Geppetto," replied the puppet.

"And does he earn much money?" asked Fire-eater.

"Much money? He hasn't a penny to his name. He even sold his only coat so that he could buy me an alphabet book."

"Poor devil!" said the puppet master with feeling. "Here are five gold sovereigns. Please take them to him at once with my compliments."

Pinocchio thanked the puppet master with all his heart. Then he said goodbye to all the other puppets and set off for home. He had not gone far down the road when he met a fox and a cat. The fox had one foot wrapped round and round with bandages and the cat seemed to be blind. Like good friends, the fox was leaning on the cat and the cat was being guided by the fox.

"Good day, Pinocchio!" said the fox politely.

"How do you know my name?" asked the puppet. "I don't know yours."

"I know your father well," replied the fox. "In fact I saw him only yesterday."

"What was he doing?" asked Pinocchio.

"Oh, he was just standing in his doorway in his shirt sleeves, shivering with the cold," said the fox.

"Poor father!" said the puppet. "Still, from now on he will never have to shiver again. Not now that we are rich."

"Rich—you?" said the fox rudely, and the cat began to laugh, hiding his smirking face by combing his whiskers with his front paws. Pinocchio was angry at this and he took out the five gold sovereigns to show them to the fox and the cat. When he heard the coins clinking together, the fox stood stock still, putting his full weight on the paw which had seemed to be so painful. The cat opened wide the eyes which had seemed to be blind—and quickly shut them again. Pinocchio was too excited about the money to notice.

"When I get home I am going to buy a new coat for my father, made of gold and silver with diamond buttons. And then I'm going to buy myself a new alphabet book."

"An alphabet book?" said the fox, looking puzzled.

"Of course!" said Pinocchio. "I'm going to go to school to learn and I'm going to work really hard."

"Oh, I wouldn't do that if I were you," said the fox. "Look at me. It was through wanting to learn that I lost the use of my leg."

"And look at me," said the cat. "It was through working too hard at my studies that I lost my sight."

At that moment a blackbird chirped up from the hedge by the side of the road: "Pinocchio, don't listen to what they say, or you will regret it!" Hearing this, the cat darted across to the hedge, lunged out at the blackbird with his paw and pulled out a pawful of feathers. Then he came back and shut his eyes again as if he were blind.

"Poor blackbird," said Pinocchio. "Why did you do that?"

Before the cat could answer, the fox said in a loud voice, "Would you like to turn your five miserable sovereigns into a thousand?"

"A thousand sovereigns!" cried Pinocchio in amazement. "Of course I would. But how is that possible?"

"You must come with us to the land of the owls," replied the fox.

"No, I can't," said Pinocchio firmly. "I must go home to my father. I have been a very bad son, and I have found out that it does not pay to be disobedient. If you only knew the terrible things that have happened to me!"

"Well, that's a pity," said the fox cunningly. "You are throwing away a fortune. By tomorrow your five sovereigns could have been two thousand."

"Two thousand sovereigns!" repeated the cat.

"No, that's impossible," said the puppet. "How does it work?"

"It's simple," said the fox. "Listen. In the land of the owls there is a magic field. In this field you must dig a hole, and in the hole you put, let's say, one gold sovereign and fill the hole with earth. Then you water it with two buckets of water and sprinkle it with two pinches of salt. During the night the gold sovereigns will grow and flower, and in the morning you will find a beautiful tree with gold sovereigns hanging from every branch."

Pinocchio was bewildered. "And how much would I get if I buried my five sovereigns in that field?" he asked.

"Every single sovereign would give you five hundred," replied the fox. "So you would get five times five hundred, that's two thousand five hundred shining gold sovereigns!"

"That's wonderful!" cried Pinocchio. "As soon as I've got the money I shall keep two thousand for myself and give the other five hundred to you two."

"To us?" said the fox as if he were offended.

"To us?" repeated the cat.

"We want nothing for ourselves," said the fox proudly. "We simply wish to help others."

"Help others," repeated the cat.

"How kind they are!" thought Pinocchio, forgetting all about his father, the new coat and the alphabet book. "Come on!" he said to the fox and the cat. "Let's go at once to the magic field. I can't wait to be rich!"

Pinocchio and the blue fairy

Pinocchio and his two new companions walked and walked, until at last they arrived at a place called the Lobster Inn. As it was already evening and they were very tired, the fox suggested that they stop at the inn to have a rest and something to eat.

When they had settled themselves at a table, the cat said that he had stomach-ache and was not feeling well—but he still managed to eat thirty-five sardines and four large portions of meat. The fox said that he couldn't eat much as his doctor had put him on a strict diet—but he still managed a hare, two plump chickens, a dish of partridge and a rabbit. But he couldn't eat anything more, he said; he simply wasn't hungry.

Pinocchio really did eat nothing. All he could think of was the magic field and a great pile of gold sovereigns. When they left the table, the fox said to the innkeeper: "Give us two good rooms, one for Mr. Pinocchio and the other for me and my friend. But don't fail to wake us at midnight."

"Yes, sir," replied the innkeeper, giving the fox a big wink to show he understood just what was going on. Pinocchio noticed nothing.

Pinocchio fell asleep as soon as his head touched the pillow. He dreamed that he was in a field full of trees, and the trees were covered in gold coins. Just as he was stretching out his hand to pick some coins from one of the trees, there was a loud knock at his door and he woke up with a start. It was the innkeeper, who had come to tell him that it was midnight.

"Are my friends ready?" asked the puppet.

"Ready and gone," replied the innkeeper. "They left two hours ago. Said they had urgent business."

"Did they pay for their supper?" asked Pinocchio.

"Good heavens, no. They wouldn't dream of insulting a gentleman like you in such a way."

"What a pity," said Pinocchio. "Did they at least leave a message?"

"Yes," said the innkeeper. "They said they would meet you at dawn in the magic field."

Pinocchio paid a sovereign for the supper and the rooms and set off at once. It was so dark that he could hardly see his hand in front of his face. There was a deathly silence across the whole countryside. Suddenly a bird flew just past Pinocchio's face and gave him a terrible fright. Then he noticed an insect crawling up a tree trunk, shining like a glow-worm.

"Who are you?" asked Pinocchio in a trembling voice.

"I am the ghost of the talking cricket," answered the insect in a very faint voice. "I have some advice for you. Go straight home with the four sovereigns that you have left. Your father is very worried about you."

"Tomorrow my father will be rich. By then these four sovereigns will have become two thousand!" said the puppet.

"Never trust those who promise to make you

rich in a day," said the cricket. "They are usually either madmen or villains. Go home at once! It's late."

"I don't care, I'm going on," said Pinocchio.

"The night is dark and cold."

"I don't care."

"The road is dangerous: there are robbers about."

"I don't care."

"Go home, Pinocchio. Remember that children who are determined to have their own way usually regret it sooner or later."

"Still the same old stories," said Pinocchio. "Good night, cricket."

"Good night, Pinocchio, and may heaven protect you from rogues and villains." Having said this, the cricket vanished as if a light had been switched off. The road ahead seemed darker than ever.

"It's not fair," said Pinocchio to himself as he went on his way. "Everyone tells us children off and tries to give us good advice. Robbers indeed! I don't believe in them. Even if I did meet them, I wouldn't be frightened. I would simply tell them not to risk messing about with me and they would go on their way. And even if they didn't, I could always run away myself."

At that moment Pinocchio thought he heard the leaves rustling behind him. He turned round and saw two shadowy figures covered from head to toe in black sacks. They were running after him on tiptoe. "Robbers!" thought Pinocchio to himself and, having nowhere to hide his gold sovereigns, he opened his mouth and put them under his tongue. Before he had run more than a few steps, something grabbed his arm in a strong grip and a horrible voice said: "Your money or your life!"

Pinocchio was unable to answer because of the money in his mouth, so by bowing and miming he tried to make the two hooded figures understand that he was just a poor puppet without as much as a penny in his pocket. "Stop dancing about and give us your money!" shouted one of the robbers. "Otherwise we shall kill you, and then we shall kill your father!"

"No, not father!" cried Pinocchio, and as he did so the sovereigns made a clinking noise in his mouth.

"Ah, so that's where you've hidden your money," said the robber. "Now hand it over or we'll make you spit it out!" As Pinocchio still said and did nothing, one robber grabbed him by the nose, the other by the chin, and they tried to force his mouth open. Quick as lightning, Pinocchio bit one of the robber's hands and was amazed to find that it was a furry paw he had between his teeth. His bite had the right effect and Pinocchio managed to free himself for a moment. Seeing his chance, he ran off as fast as he could.

The two robbers chased him and although Pinocchio managed to keep a few paces ahead, after a few miles he was nearly exhausted. On and on he ran until, to his horror, he found his way barred by a deep ditch full of dirty water. Taking a long run-up, he leaped straight across the ditch and landed safely on the other side. The two robbers failed to judge the distance so well, and—splash! splash!—they both landed in the dirty water.

Pinocchio laughed. "Enjoy your bath!" he shouted as he ran off again. But when he looked back a few moments later, there they were, chasing after him, with water dripping everywhere from their soaking black sacks.

Ahead lay a dark forest and Pinocchio plunged headlong into the undergrowth. Still he could hear the robbers chasing along behind. He was by now so tired that he felt like sitting down and allowing them to take all his money. Fortunately, just as he was about to give up, he spotted a small white house in a distant clearing. "If I could just manage to reach that house," he thought, "I might be saved." And on he ran, faster than ever.

When at last Pinocchio arrived at the little white house, he was quite out of breath. He knocked urgently on the door. No-one answered. Pinocchio could hear the two robbers coming nearer and he knocked again with all his strength. When there was still no reply, he began to bang and kick the door, until finally a window opened and he saw the face of a beautiful young girl. She had blue hair and spoke in a faint voice: "There is no-one here except me, and I am not of this world." With this she disappeared and the window closed again without a sound.

"Oh please help me!" cried Pinocchio. "I am being chased by two terrible robb . . . " Before he could finish the word, he was grabbed from behind by four strong arms.

"This time you won't escape!" said a voice. "Open your mouth or you're done for!" Pinocchio was so frightened that he began to tremble violently and his wooden joints began to creak. But he would not open his mouth. The robbers beat him with sticks but, as he was made of very hard wood, the sticks simply broke into little pieces.

The two robbers were furious. "It's no good," one of them said, "we'll have to go and get some knives. Let's tie him up in the meantime." So they tied his hands and feet with strong rope and dragged him off to the edge of the forest. "When we return, perhaps you will already be dead—if we are lucky," said one of the robbers in a horrible voice as they left.

After a while a strong wind began to blow and heavy drops of rain fell through the branches of the forest trees. Poor Pinocchio was tied so tightly that he could not move at all and he lay there shivering as the storm raged around. "Oh father, if only you were here now!" he said softly to himself, feeling weaker and more sorry for himself than ever.

While Pinocchio was lying there in despair, the beautiful girl with blue hair came again to the window. She peered into the dark forest and saw the puppet, looking like a sad bundle of wet sticks. Feeling sorry for him, she clapped her hands three times. At this signal there was a sound of flapping wings and a huge falcon flew onto the window-sill.

"What is your command, gracious fairy?" asked the falcon, for the beautiful girl with blue hair was not an ordinary girl at all but a fairy who had lived in that house for more than a thousand years.

"Fly to the puppet," she replied, "and with your strong beak break the knots that keep him tied up." The falcon obeyed and then returned to the fairy.

"Is the puppet still alive?" she asked.

"At first he appeared to be dead," said the falcon. "But when I loosened the ropes, I heard him mutter 'Now I feel better'. I think he'll live." The fairy then clapped her hands twice and a large poodle appeared, walking on his hind legs like a man. He was dressed as a coachman with a curly white wig and a three-cornered hat on his head. He had a chocolate-coloured waistcoat with diamond buttons and two large pockets to keep his bones in, a pair of red velvet breeches, silk stockings and a blue satin umbrella case to put his tail into when it rained.

"Be quick, Medoro, like a good dog!" said the fairy. "Prepare my best carriage and drive it to the forest. There you will find a puppet, lying half dead. Place him in the carriage very gently and bring him here to me."

The poodle ran off and shortly afterwards drove up to the house with Pinocchio lying unconscious on the back seat of the carriage.

The fairy herself took Pinocchio in her arms and carried him into the little white house.

Pinocchio tells a lie

The fairy called for the three best doctors in the district, who happened to be a crow, an owl and a cricket. When they arrived, the fairy told them that she wanted to know if the puppet was truly still alive. The crow stepped forward and felt Pinocchio's pulse. Then he felt his nose, then his little toe. At last he said solemnly, "I do believe the puppet is dead, but if indeed he is not dead, then it would be a sign that he is still alive!"

"I am afraid," said the owl, "that I must disagree with my learned friend. I believe the puppet is alive, but if indeed he is not alive, then it would be a sign that he is definitely dead!"

"And what do you have to say?" the fairy asked the cricket.

"I believe that a wise doctor should keep quiet when he doesn't know what he is talking about. But for myself, I have met this puppet before and I know him well!" At this Pinocchio was seized with a fit of trembling that shook the whole bed. "That puppet," continued the cricket, "is a good-for-nothing." Pinocchio quickly opened his eyes, but shut them again immediately. "He is a ragamuffin and a lazybones. And what's more, he is a disobedient son who will cause his poor father to die of a broken heart."

Pinocchio had hidden his face beneath the bedclothes and now a distinct sound of sobbing came from the bed.

"When a dead person cries," said the crow wisely, "it is a sign that he is getting better."

"I am afraid," said the owl, "that I must disagree with my learned friend. When a dead person cries, it is definitely a sign that he does not want to die!"

When the three doctors had left, the fairy felt Pinocchio's forehead and found that he really did have a high temperature. She went straight to a cupboard and took out some white powder, which she stirred into a glass of water.

"Drink this," she said gently to Pinocchio, "and in a few days you will be better."

Pinocchio looked at the glass and pulled a face. "Is it sweet or bitter?" he asked.

"It is slightly bitter, but it will do you good," said the fairy.

"But I can't drink anything bitter."

"Drink it and then I'll give you a lump of sugar to take away the taste."

"Give me the sugar lump first and then I promise I'll drink it."

The fairy gave Pinocchio a sugar lump and he ate it at once. Then she gave him the glass again. He sniffed at it, started to put it to his lips, sniffed at it again, and finally he said, "It's too bitter! I can't drink it!"

"How do you know when you haven't even tasted it?" asked the fairy patiently.

"I can tell from the smell. Give me another

lump of sugar first, and then I'll drink it." The fairy gave him another lump of sugar and then handed him the glass again.

"I can't drink it like this!" said the puppet. "The pillow on my feet is bothering me." So the fairy took the pillow away.

"It's still no good," said Pinocchio. "There's a draught from the door!" So the fairy shut the door.

Pinocchio burst into tears. "I can't drink that bitter medicine," he cried. "I can't!"

"You'll never get better if you don't take your medicine," said the fairy kindly.

"I don't care," said the puppet. "I'd rather die than drink that bitter medicine!"

At that moment the door of the room flew open and in came four black rabbits, carrying a coffin on their shoulders. "Good day," said the first rabbit. "We have come to take you away."

Pinocchio sat up in bed, feeling very frightened. "Take me away?" he said. "But why? I'm not dead!"

"Ah but you soon will be," said the second rabbit, "if you refuse to take your medicine!"

"Fairy, fairy!" cried Pinocchio. "Bring the medicine, give it to me, I don't want to die!" And taking the glass in both hands, he drank the medicine down at once. When they saw this, the rabbits simply turned round and left the room, with the coffin still on their shoulders. Pinocchio heaved a sigh of relief and a few minutes later jumped out of bed feeling quite well. You see, wooden puppets are rarely ill and are cured very quickly.

"There you are, you're better already," said the fairy, as Pinocchio ran and jumped round the room. "Now why did you have to be persuaded to take the medicine?"

"Because all us children are like that," replied Pinocchio. "We are more afraid of the medicine than of being ill! But next time I won't have to be persuaded. I shall think of those black rabbits with the coffin and take my medicine straightaway!"

"Good. Now come here to me," said the fairy, "and tell me how you fell into the hands of those robbers."

"Well, you see it was like this," said the puppet. "The puppet master Fire-eater gave me some gold sovereigns and told me to take them to my father and instead I met a fox and a cat and they said they could make the sovereigns into a thousand or two in the magic field and I went with them and we stopped at the Lobster Inn and when I woke up they had gone and I went after them and it was very dark and I met the two robbers who wanted my money, but I had hidden it in my mouth, and I bit one of them on the hand and instead of a hand it was a furry paw and they chased after me and I ran and ran until at last they caught me and they tied me up and said they would come back tomorrow and hoped I'd be dead."

"And where are the gold sovereigns now?" asked the fairy.

"I've lost them," said Pinocchio, though he had them in his pocket all the time. As soon as he said this, his funny, turned-up nose grew at least four centimetres longer.

"Where did you lose them?"

"In the forest." At this second lie Pinocchio's nose grew even longer.

"That's all right then," said the fairy, "because everything that is lost in that forest is always found."

"Oh wait a minute, now I remember," said the puppet. "I didn't lose them, I swallowed them by mistake when I was drinking the medicine." At this third lie his nose grew so long that he could hardly move at all. When he turned his head, trying to hide his face, his nose bumped against the wall. The fairy looked at him and laughed, and Pinocchio felt very embarrassed.

"What are you laughing at?" he asked.

"I'm laughing at the lies you tell," replied the fairy.

"How do you know that I'm telling lies?" he asked.

"Because lies are found out at once," she said. "There are two kinds of lies, those with short legs and those with long noses. And your lies happen to have a very long nose!"

Pinocchio did not know what to do with himself, he felt so silly. He could not even run out of the room: his nose was so big that he was frightened of getting it stuck fast in the doorway! Pinocchio began to cry.

Buried treasure

The fairy allowed Pinocchio to cry for half an hour to teach him a lesson about telling lies but at last she could no longer bear to hear his sobs and see his unhappy, swollen face. She clapped her hands once and immediately hundreds of woodpeckers flew in through the window. A whole group of them perched on Pinocchio's nose and began to peck at it so furiously that within a few minutes his enormous nose was back to its normal size.

"Oh thank you, fairy," said Pinocchio. "What a good friend you are!"

"I am indeed your friend," answered the fairy, "and if you will stay here with me, you can be my little brother."

"I would love to," said the puppet. "But what about my poor father?"

"I have already thought of that," the fairy said. "Your father knows all about you and will be here tonight."

Pinocchio jumped for joy and asked the fairy if he could go some of the way to meet his father; he was so anxious to see him. She said that he should take the road through the forest, but he must be very careful not to get lost.

Pinocchio set off at once and as soon as he came to the edge of the forest he began to run as fast as he could. When he reached the spot where he had been tied up, he heard two voices in the bushes and was astonished to see his two former companions, the fox and the cat.

"Why, it's our good friend Pinocchio!" cried the fox, throwing his arms round the puppet. "How do you come to be here?"

"That's a long story," replied Pinocchio. "But you know when you left me the other night, well I met two robbers on the road. They tried to steal my gold sovereigns."

"Robbers!" said the fox.

"Robbers!" repeated the cat.

Then Pinocchio told them how he had been tied up and left to die. "What a dreadful story!" said the fox. "Is it no longer possible for peace-loving people like us to live in safety?"

While they were talking, Pinocchio noticed that the cat had a bandage round one of his front paws. When he asked him what had happened, the cat started to stutter and the fox said hurriedly: "My friend is too modest to tell you what happened. An hour ago we met an old wolf on the road who said he was starving. Naturally our friend here went to give him his last fishbone, and all he got for his trouble was a nasty bite on the paw! But tell us, where are you going?"

Pinocchio explained that he was meeting his father. "And your gold sovereigns?" asked the fox.

"They are here in my pocket, except for the one I spent at the inn."

"And to think they could be one or two thousand!" said the fox. "You could still take my advice and go and bury them in the magic field."

"I can't go today," said the puppet quickly. "I'll go another day."

"But another day will be too late!" cried the fox. "The field has just been sold and after tomorrow nobody will be allowed to bury money there. So please change your mind. The field is less than two miles away, we can be there in half an hour. By tomorrow you could be rich. Won't you come with us?"

Pinocchio hesitated. He thought of the good

fairy, his father, and the cricket's warnings, but in the end he said to the fox and the cat, "Let's go!" And off they went. After walking for a time they reached a town called Blockheadsville, where the streets were crowded with dogs who had lost their coats, sheep without wool, butterflies with no wings, peacocks without their tails and pheasants who had lost their brilliant feathers.

"Where is the magic field?" asked Pinocchio.

"Just over there," replied the fox. There, on the other side of the town, was a field which looked just like any other field.

"This is it," said the fox. "Quickly now. Just dig a small hole with your hands and put the four sovereigns in." Pinocchio did as he was told, and then covered the hole over with earth.

"Now go over to that canal," said the fox, "and fetch a can of water." Pinocchio went to the canal and, having no can, filled one of his shoes with water. Then he watered the ground where the hole was.

"Now we must go," said the fox. "When you come back in twenty minutes you will find a shrub with its branches loaded with money!" Pinocchio thanked the fox and the cat and promised them each a present.

"We want no presents," said the fox, grinning all over his face. "It is enough for us to have taught you how to make money without working at all."

"Without working at all," repeated the cat.

And with that they went on their way.

Pinocchio went back to the town and counted the minutes one by one. When he reached twenty, he returned to the magic field. His heart was beating fast and he thought to himself, "What if instead of a thousand sovereigns there are a hundred thousand? How rich I'd be! I'd have a beautiful palace, a thousand little wooden horses, and tins and tins of sweets, cakes and biscuits!"

When he reached the field, he was surprised not to be able to see the money tree at once. Thinking it must still be quite small, he went right up to the spot where he had buried the sovereigns, but there was nothing there. Pinocchio could not understand it. He was

standing there scratching his head, when suddenly he heard the sound of laughter close by. Looking up, he saw a large, brightly coloured but rather scruffy parrot preening his battered feathers.

"Why are you laughing?" Pinocchio asked the parrot.

"I tickled myself preening my feathers," replied the parrot.

Pinocchio just shook his head and went to the canal to fill his shoe with water again. When he started watering the earth once more, there was another loud laugh. Pinocchio was furious. "Once and for all," he shouted at the parrot, "tell me what you are laughing at!"

"Well, if you must know," said the parrot in his croaky voice, "I am laughing at fools who believe the stupid things they are told and who get caught out by cunning crooks."

"And are you referring to me by any chance?" asked the puppet.

"Yes, poor Pinocchio, I am," said the parrot. "You were foolish enough to believe that money could grow on trees. I also believed it once, just like all the other fools who now live in Blockheadsville, and today we are all suffering for it. Now I know that it is better to earn a few pennies honestly, by using your hands or your brain. You will learn this too. You might as well know that while you were in the town the fox and the cat came back and took the money that you buried. Then they ran off as fast as they could. You'd have to be very clever to catch them now."

Pinocchio was stunned. He just could not believe what he had heard and he started to dig up the earth frantically with his hands and nails.

He went on digging till he could practically stand up in the hole, but the gold sovereigns had gone. Pinocchio rushed back to the town and went straight to the police station.

He told the station officer how he had been robbed by two villains and a policeman led him before the judge at the nearby law courts. The judge was a huge gorilla with a white beard and gold spectacles. Pinocchio told the gorilla the whole story of how he had been misled, giving a full description of the two robbers. The judge listened to the story very carefully and patiently. When Pinocchio had finished, he reached out his hand and rang a little bell.

Two guard-dogs immediately appeared, dressed as policemen. The judge pointed to Pinocchio and said to the dogs: "This poor devil has been robbed of four gold sovereigns. Take him and put him straight into prison."

Pinocchio could not believe his ears. He tried to protest, but the policemen quickly gagged him and led him off to prison. And there he remained for four long months.

He would probably have been in prison for even longer, but he was finally released by a lucky chance. The young prince who ruled over the district had won a great victory over his enemies and, to celebrate his triumph, he ordered that all prisoners should be set free. At first the jailor told Pinocchio that he was not one of the lucky ones, but the puppet protested strongly.

"I beg your pardon," he said, "but I am also a criminal."

At this the jailor took off his hat, bowed graciously, opened the prison gates and set Pinocchio free.

Pinocchio meets a snake

Pinocchio was overjoyed to be free again. He decided to leave the town immediately and took the road that led to the fairy's house.

Because of the rainy weather the road had become like a marsh and Pinocchio sank down to his knees as he hurried along. Before long he was covered in mud from head to toe but this did not bother him. He was too anxious to see his father and his new sister again. As he ran along, he said to himself "What a terrible time I've had. But I deserve it! I've been disobedient, always wanting my own way, never listening to those with more sense than me. But from now on, things are going to be different. I've learned my lesson. Oh how I long to see my father and the fairy again. How I love them both! What an ungrateful wretch I've been!"

Suddenly Pinocchio stopped in his tracks. There, right in front of him, was a huge snake, lying across the road. Its body was green and scaly, its head many-coloured with fiery red eyes and it had a pointed tail that was smoking like a factory chimney. Pinocchio was terrified. He crept away to a safe distance and sat down on a pile of stones to wait for the snake to slither away. He waited one hour, two hours, three hours, but the snake did not stir. Even from his safe distance, Pinocchio could see the snake's red eyes glowing and the column of smoke rising from the end of its tail. At last Pinocchio summoned up all his courage, went a bit closer to the snake and said in a soft voice: "Excuse me, Mr. Snake sir, but would you mind moving over a bit so that I can get past?"

There was no reply and the snake still did not move. Pinocchio spoke again in the same soft, polite voice: "The fact is, Mr. Snake, sir, I am on my way home and my father is waiting for me. It's such a long time since I saw him and I know he must be anxious. If you would just move over a bit, I could pass by easily."

He waited for some sign that the snake had heard but again nothing happened except that this time the snake went quite rigid and closed

its red eyes. The smoke from its tail stopped suddenly, as if a shutter had been closed.

"Perhaps he's dead," thought Pinocchio and he decided to risk jumping over the snake while it lay so still. Just as he was about to take off, however, the snake raised its horrible head to strike and Pinocchio was so surprised and frightened that he tripped and fell over. He fell so heavily that he stuck fast in the mud and lay there kicking his legs as hard as he could to try to free himself.

Seeing this, the snake went into a fit of laughter. It laughed and laughed till it could not stop and in the end it spluttered and roared so much that it burst its lungs with a great bang. The explosion blew the mud from Pinocchio's body and, struggling to his feet, he jumped over the snake without waiting to see whether it was dead or alive and ran off down the road.

Before long Pinocchio began to feel terribly hungry and he left the road and went into a nearby field to pick some grapes. He was just about to reach out his hand for a juicy bunch of grapes when there was a horrible clanking sound. One of Pinocchio's legs was trapped between two sharp iron bars that had sprung together. He had been caught in a trap put there to catch the wolves and polecats that stole chickens from the local farmers.

Pinocchio began to cry. The trap hurt his leg and he felt frightened out in the fields all by himself. The field, however, was deserted and there was no-one to hear him crying. At last, as it began to grow dark, a firefly came flitting above his head.

"Oh, you poor boy!" said the firefly. "How ever did you get caught in that trap?"

"I was only going to pick a few grapes," replied Pinocchio.

"And who said that you could take them?" asked the firefly.

"No-one," said Pinocchio, feeling worse than ever, "but I was so hungry and I promise I'll never do it again."

Before he could say any more, Pinocchio heard the sound of heavy footsteps. It was the farmer who owned the field, coming to see what was caught in his trap. He was expecting to find a wolf or a polecat, so he was very surprised when he saw Pinocchio. "Ah, a thief!" shouted the farmer. "So it's you who steals my chickens every night!"

"No, it's not me, I don't steal chickens," sobbed Pinocchio. "I was only going to pick a few grapes."

"Someone who steals grapes is just as likely to steal chickens!" said the farmer. "I can see I'll have to teach you a lesson!" Saying this, the farmer opened the trap, grabbed Pinocchio and dragged him off to the farmhouse. When they got there, the farmer put a big collar around Pinocchio's neck. There was a heavy chain attached to the collar and this was fastened to a post.

"There you are, young thief," he said. "My old guard-dog died today, so you can take his place for the night. If it rains, you can shelter in the dog's kennel and if any robbers come, make sure you bark nice and loudly. Remember, you're my watch-dog now!" With this the farmer went into the house and locked the door.

Pinocchio lay on the ground, feeling cold, hungry and very frightened. He felt the heavy collar round his neck and sobbed, "It's my own fault, it serves me right! I've been stupid and listened to foolish stories. If I had been a good boy, willing to learn and work, and if I had stayed at home with my poor father, then I wouldn't have to be a farmer's watch-dog. If only I could start all over again. But now it's too late!"

Pinocchio meant everything he said. He could see no way to escape and it was quite clear that everything was his own fault. Once he had realized this he felt a little better and, quite exhausted by fear and crying, he crept into the kennel and fell fast asleep.

He slept soundly for a couple of hours but then, towards midnight, he was woken by strange whispering voices. Peeping out of the kennel, he saw four little animals pointing and whispering to each other. They were polecats. One of them crept up to the kennel and said in a low voice, "Hello, Melampo, how are you tonight?"

"My name is not Melampo," said Pinocchio

in a loud voice, "it is Pinocchio."

"Where's old Melampo then?" asked the polecat.

"Dead," replied Pinocchio.

"Poor old Melampo!" whispered the polecat. "Still, I can see from your face that you're a friendly dog."

"I am not a dog!" said Pinocchio. "I am a puppet, and I am only acting as watch-dog as a punishment. Now what do you want?"

"What do we want?" asked the polecat quietly. "Why, the same as always, and we'll offer you the same conditions as poor old Melampo. You let us visit the chicken run and carry off eight chickens. We'll give you one of the chickens as long as you pretend to be asleep and don't on any account wake the farmer."

"Did Melampo allow you in?" asked Pinocchio.

"Certainly," replied the polecat, "and it always worked out well. Just pretend to be asleep and we will leave a beautiful chicken by the kennel, ready plucked for your breakfast tomorrow morning. Understand?"

"Oh perfectly," said the puppet.

The four polecats then went straight off to the chicken run and started to pick away at the wooden gate with their teeth and claws. When it opened they slipped in one after the other. As soon as they were in, they heard the gate slam shut behind them. Pinocchio had crept along and closed it, putting a big stone against it to keep it firmly closed. Then he began to bark and howl like a dog, as loudly as he could.

The barking woke the farmer at once and he ran to the window with his gun in his hands. "What's going on?" he shouted.

"There are thieves in the chicken run," Pinocchio shouted back.

The farmer rushed out of the house and went straight to the chicken run. He caught the four polecats easily and put them in a large sack. "At last I've caught you!" he said. "In the morning I shall take you to the innkeeper, and he will skin and cook you like hares. Even that's more than you deserve!" Then he turned to Pinocchio. "Well done, young sir! But how did you manage to catch them? Melampo certainly never did."

Pinocchio was tempted to tell him the whole story, but he remembered that the dog was dead and he thought it was best to leave him in peace. "The polecats woke me up with their whispering," he said, "and when they realized that I was awake one of them had the cheek to ask me to promise not to bark! I may be a puppet and a naughty one at that, but there is one thing you can't accuse me of, and that is helping crooks and thieves!"

"Good boy!" cried the farmer, patting Pinocchio on the back. "I am most grateful to you and, as a sign of my gratitude, I shall let you go at once." With this he took off Pinocchio's collar, shook him by the hand and sent him on his way with a hunk of bread and a large wedge of cheese.

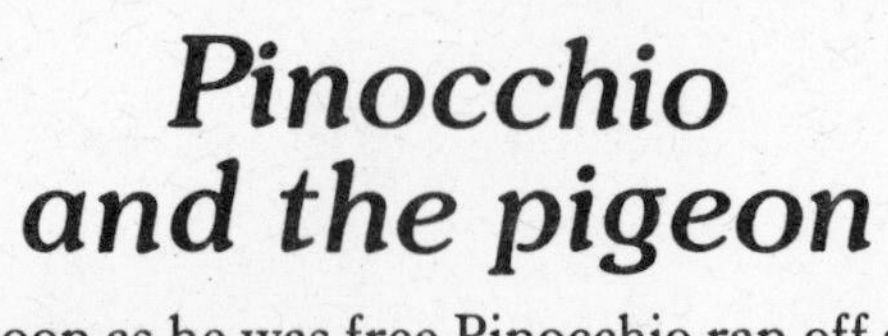

Pinocchio and the pigeon

As soon as he was free Pinocchio ran off across the fields to the road that led to the fairy's house. Before long he could see in the distance the forest where he had been tied up, but there was no sign of the little white house. This made Pinocchio anxious and he began to run even faster.

When at last he reached the field where the house had once stood, he was astonished to find that it was indeed no longer there. In its place was a marble stone, and, remembering

some of the letters he had learned in prison, he managed to read the sad words engraved on it:

HERE LIES THE
BEAUTIFUL GIRL WITH
BLUE HAIR WHO LOST
HER LITTLE BROTHER
PINOCCHIO AND DIED OF
A BROKEN HEART.

The poor little puppet burst into tears and threw himself on the ground next to the marble stone. He cried all night long and next morning he was still crying, though he had no tears left. As he wept, he said to himself, "Poor little fairy, why did you die? Why couldn't I die instead of you? You were so good and I am so worthless. And what about my father? Where can he be? Oh come alive again little fairy, and tell me where to find him. If you really love me, don't leave me alone in the world. Who will give me food? Where shall I sleep? It would be best if I were dead too!"

Just then a large pigeon flew over Pinocchio's head and called down to him: "Tell me, child, do you happen to know a puppet called Pinocchio?"

"I am Pinocchio," replied the puppet and the pigeon immediately flew down and landed right beside him.

"Do you know Geppetto as well?" asked the pigeon.

"Know him?" said Pinocchio. "He is my dear father. Why, have you seen him?"

"I left him three days ago at the seashore," said the pigeon. "He was building himself a little boat so that he could cross the ocean to try to find you. He has been looking for you everywhere."

"How far is it to the seashore?" asked Pinocchio, hardly able to contain his excitement.

"A very long way. More than six hundred miles. But if you want to go, I will carry you there on my back."

Pinocchio agreed at once and, thanking the pigeon, clambered up onto his back. They flew off and in a few minutes had soared so high that they almost touched the clouds. Pinocchio was curious to see what the ground looked like from up there but the height made him feel so dizzy that he looked up again quickly and wound his arms even more tightly around the pigeon's neck.

They flew all day without stopping, and towards evening the pigeon said that he felt thirsty. "Let's stop for a few minutes at that bird-house. Then we'll carry on so that we reach the seashore by dawn tomorrow." When they got to the bird-house, they found nothing but a bowl of water and a basket full of beans. Pinocchio had never been able to eat beans before, as he said they made him sick, but that evening he ate them till he was full. "I never knew that beans tasted so good!" he said to the pigeon.

"Take it from me," replied the pigeon, "all food tastes good when you are really hungry."

Off they went again and next morning at dawn they reached the seashore. When they had landed, Pinocchio climbed down from the pigeon's back but, before he could even say thank you, the pigeon flew off and disappeared. There was a crowd of people on the shore, shouting and waving at something. Pinocchio asked an old woman what was going on.

"A poor father who has lost his son has set off in a little boat to cross the ocean," she replied, "but the sea is so rough today that the boat is in danger of sinking. Look, there it is!" And she pointed to the boat, which was very far away, bobbing about like a cork. By screwing up his eyes against the glare and looking very hard, Pinocchio could just see a figure sitting in the boat.

"It's my father!" he shouted at the top of his voice. "Father! Father! Can you hear me?" Pinocchio jumped and waved, and it seemed as if Geppetto recognized him, because he took off his cap and waved back. But the sea was so choppy that he was unable to use his oars to row back to shore.

Suddenly a huge wave came up and the little

boat disappeared. They all waited, hoping to see the boat again, but it did not reappear. "Poor man!" said the old woman quietly. Just then she heard a shout from the rocks. It was Pinocchio.

"I must rescue my father!" he shouted, and dived into the sea from a large rock.

As he was made of wood, Pinocchio floated easily and could swim like a fish but the sea was so rough that he often disappeared from the sight of those still watching from the shore. Time after time he reappeared, his arms and legs kicking out wildly. "Poor boy," said the old woman. At last he was too far out for anyone to see his small body among the waves and the crowd of watchers gradually made their way home.

The Island of Busy Bees

Pinocchio swam all night; and what a terrible night it was. It poured with rain, the thunder and lightning roared and flashed and the wind whipped the waves into great hills and valleys. Every time he was tossed onto the crest of a wave, Pinocchio peered as far as he could over the sea, but he saw no sign of his father's little boat. Towards morning he saw a long strip of land in the distance; it was an island in the middle of the sea.

As he swam nearer the shore, a great wave suddenly took hold of him, lifted him up and hurled him on to the sand. The fall made his wooden joints creak but he was pleased to be on land again. As he lay getting his breath back, the sky gradually cleared, the sun came out and the sea became calm. Pinocchio put his soaking clothes out in the sun to dry and began to look out to sea in the hope of spotting a little boat. There was nothing but sea and sky.

"If only I knew what this island was called," he said to himself. Realizing that he was all alone, he began to feel very sad again but just as he was about to start crying, he saw a dolphin swimming close to the shore. "Excuse me, Mr. Dolphin sir, but could I have a word with you?" he shouted.

"Certainly," replied the dolphin. "You can have two if you like!"

"Would you be kind enough to tell me if there is anywhere on this island where I could get something to eat without running the risk of being tied up or put in prison or killed?" Pinocchio asked in his politest voice.

"Certainly," said the dolphin again. "There is a village nearby. Just follow that path to your left, you can't go wrong."

"And another thing," said the puppet. "Do you happen to have seen a little boat with a man in it? You see, I've lost my father."

"I'm afraid the boat must have sunk to the bottom during last night's storm," replied the dolphin. "And your father must have been swallowed by the terrible dogfish who has been causing havoc in these waters recently."

"Is this dogfish very big?" asked Pinocchio, feeling frightened already.

"Big?" cried the dolphin. "He is bigger than a five-storey house, and his mouth is so huge that a railway train could pass down his throat!" With that the dolphin swam away.

Pinocchio had already dressed and now he hurried off down the path the dolphin had pointed out. He was so nervous that at the slightest noise he looked behind him, fearing that he might see the terrible dogfish following him with a train roaring out of its mouth. After half an hour he was relieved to reach the village. On a sign beside the first house were the words "Village of Busy Bees". Everywhere there were people rushing about busily doing things.

"This village will never suit me," thought the lazy Pinocchio. "I wasn't born to work!" But he knew he would have to do something because he was once again feeling very hungry indeed. He would either have to work or beg. His father had taught him that no-one had the right to beg except the old and the sick, who are unable to earn money by their own hands. Everyone else has a duty to work, his father had always said. However, Pinocchio had never taken much notice of good advice!

While he was wondering what to do next, a man came down the road pulling two carts full of coal. Pinocchio looked down and said in a quiet voice: "Would you please be kind enough to give me a halfpenny, for I am dying of hunger."

"I will not *give* you a halfpenny," replied the man, "but I will *pay* you twopence if you will help me take these two carts of coal home."

"Really!" said the puppet in an offended voice. "I must tell you that I am not used to doing a donkey's work!"

"Well, good for you!" said the man. "If you are dying of hunger, you had better eat two slices of your pride and be careful you don't get stomach-ache!"

A few minutes later a builder came down the road carrying a large tin of cement. "Would you please be kind enough to give a halfpenny to a poor boy who is weak from lack of food?" asked Pinocchio quietly.

"If you'll carry this cement for me," answered the builder, "I'll pay you fivepence."

"But the cement looks very heavy," said Pinocchio, "and I don't want to tire myself out."

"In that case you'd better stay here, though it won't do you any good," said the builder angrily.

In less than half an hour another twenty people went by and Pinocchio begged all of them for money, but always with the same result. Then a nice little woman carrying two cans of water came past. "May I have a drink of water?" asked Pinocchio.

"Drink as much as you like!" replied the little woman, putting down the cans. Pinocchio picked up one of the cans and took a long drink. Then he said quietly, "I'm not thirsty any more now. If only I were not still hungry."

The little woman heard this and said, "If you will help me to carry these two cans of water home, I will give you a lovely piece of bread."

Pinocchio took a long look at the cans. "And as well as the bread, you can have a nice bowl of strawberries," the little woman added.

Pinocchio took another look at the cans. "And as well as the strawberries, you can have a big slice of chocolate pudding."

The temptation of the chocolate pudding

was too much for the puppet, and he agreed to carry the cans. They were so heavy that he had to stop and rest several times on the way. As soon as they reached the little woman's house she sat Pinocchio down at a small table that was already laid and brought him the bread, strawberries and chocolate pudding. Pinocchio was so hungry that he gobbled down the food in no time. Then at last he looked up to thank the little woman. Noticing her properly for the first time, he just stared, his eyes wide and round with astonishment.

"What is it?" asked the little woman.

"It's . . . it's . . . " stammered Pinocchio, "it's just that you remind me so much . . . the same voice . . . the same eyes . . . and the same blue hair . . . oh fairy, tell me that it's really you! Please don't make me cry any more! If only you knew how much I've cried!" And throwing himself at the little woman's feet, he put his arms round her knees and started to cry.

At first the little woman would not admit that she was the fairy but then she said to Pinocchio: "You little rascal! How did you find me out? When you left I was just a child, and now I'm a grown-up woman, almost old enough to be your mother."

"It's because I love you so much that I know who you are," replied Pinocchio. "And now instead of calling you sister, I shall call you mother. I have always wanted to have a mother like other children. But how did you manage to grow so fast?"

"That's a secret," replied the fairy.

"Please tell me the secret," begged Pinocchio. "I am still very small and I would like to grow into a man as quickly as possible."

"But you are a puppet," said the fairy, "and puppets never grow. However, you could become a boy if you deserved it."

"Really? And what do I have to do to deserve it?" asked the puppet.

"It's easy really," said the fairy. "You must learn to be good. Good boys are obedient and you . . . "

"And I never obey," interrupted Pinocchio.

"Good boys like to learn and work and you . . . "

"And I am a lazybones."

"Good boys always tell the truth . . . "

"And I tell lies."

"Good boys go to school . . . "

"And the thought of school gives me a pain all over. But from today I'll be different. I promise that I'll be a good little boy and look after my father. Do you know where he is?"

"No," replied the fairy, "but I'm sure you will see him again before long."

Pinocchio was so delighted at this that he gave the fairy a kiss. "Tell me, mother," he said, "wasn't it true, then, that you were dead?"

"It seems not," replied the fairy, smiling.

"If only you knew how I felt," said the puppet, "when I read the words on that marble stone!"

"I know," said the fairy. "And that is why I have forgiven you. I saw that you have a good heart and that there is hope for you in spite of all your bad habits! That is why I came back to be your mother. But from now on you must do everything I say."

"Oh I will, I will!" cried Pinocchio.

"Good. Tomorrow you will start school. Then later you must find some work that you would like to do. Now why are you muttering to yourself?"

"I was just thinking," said Pinocchio seriously, "that it's too late for me to start school now, and I don't really want to find work."

"And why not?" asked the fairy angrily.

"Because work tires me out," replied Pinocchio weakly.

"People who talk like that," said the fairy, "usually end up in prison or in hospital. You must learn, my boy, that everyone has to work in this world. Laziness is a terrible thing and must be cured at once while you are still a child. Lazy adults can never be cured."

The fairy's serious words impressed Pinocchio. "I really will study and work," he said quickly. "I will do everything you say. I'm tired of being a puppet, and I'd give anything to become a boy. You did promise I could, didn't you?"

"I did promise," said the fairy kindly, "but now it's up to you."

Pinocchio goes to school

Next day Pinocchio went to school. All the other boys were delighted when they saw a puppet at school and they laughed and played all sorts of tricks on him. One boy pulled off his cap, another tried to paint a black moustache under his nose, another even tried to tie strings to his hands and feet to make him dance. Pinocchio put up with this for a while, but eventually he lost patience and shouted at the boys to stop making fun of him or they would regret it.

Hearing this, one of the boys reached out to grab Pinocchio by the nose, but the puppet was too quick for him and kicked him hard on the shins. "Ouch! What hard feet!" cried the boy. "And what hard elbows!" cried another, who received a sharp blow in the stomach. The way Pinocchio stood up for himself made all the boys like and respect him and even the teacher liked him because he was so hard-working. As the days passed, he was always the first to arrive at school and the last to leave at the end of the day.

Both the teacher and Pinocchio's mother, the blue fairy, were worried that he was now making too *many* friends. Some of the boys at school were very lazy, and the fairy warned Pinocchio constantly, "Be careful, Pinocchio. Those bad boys will lead you into trouble sooner or later."

"There's no chance of that," replied Pinocchio. "I'm much too clever!"

A few days later Pinocchio met several of his schoolfriends on his way to school. "Have you heard the news?" they asked. "A gigantic dogfish has been seen in the sea near here. He's as big as a mountain! We're going to have a look at him—do you want to come?"

Pinocchio wondered if this could be the same dogfish as the one the dolphin had mentioned when his father disappeared. But he decided that he had better go to school. "Besides," he said, "what would the teacher say, or my mother?"

"Don't worry about them!" said one of the boys. "Teachers are paid to moan and mothers don't know anything!"

"I'll tell you what," said Pinocchio suddenly. "I'll go and see the dogfish after school."

"Don't be silly," replied the boy. "Do you think a great big fish like that will wait for you? By this afternoon he'll be gone, and anyway we could be there and back in an hour."

Pinocchio hesitated. "All right then," he said at last. "Let's go! And the first one there's the winner!" Off they ran, with Pinocchio in the lead. He was easily the fastest and every now and then he would turn round to laugh at the others and tell them what slow-coaches they were. Little did Pinocchio know what dangers and troubles lay ahead of him!

When they arrived at the seashore, the sea was calm and smooth and there was no dogfish to be seen. Pinocchio turned to the boys and asked where the dogfish was. "He's probably having his breakfast," said one boy, laughing. "Or he's lying on his bed having a snooze!" laughed another.

When he saw them all laughing, Pinocchio realized that they were making a fool of him. "Why did you tell me this nonsense about a dogfish?" he asked.

"To make you miss school," answered one of the boys. "You should be ashamed of yourself, always arriving on time and working so hard. It's not fair on the rest of us, making us look so bad compared with you. So you'd better learn to change your ways!"

"And how am I supposed to do that?" asked Pinocchio with an angry look.

"By learning to hate school, lessons and the teacher—our three worst enemies. And if you don't, we'll make you pay for it!"

"Oh really?" said Pinocchio, shaking his head. "Don't make me laugh!"

This annoyed the boys intensely, and the biggest of them reminded Pinocchio that there was one of him and seven of them.

"Oh, the seven deadly sins!" laughed the puppet.

"You're asking for it!" said the boy.

"Nincompoop!" cried Pinocchio.

"I'll show you who's a nincompoop!" the boy shouted. "Take that!" And he punched Pinocchio hard on the chin. The puppet immediately returned the punch and within seconds a general fight had developed. Although he had no-one on his side, Pinocchio fought well and the other boys were soon covered in bruises from his hard wooden feet. Furious at not being able to beat him, they took their schoolbooks out of their satchels and threw these at him. Still Pinocchio was too quick and always managed to duck just in time. When they had thrown all their own books at him one of the boys noticed Pinocchio's satchel lying on the ground and he quickly snatched it up and opened it. Inside was one particularly large and heavy book, Pinocchio's reading book. The boy took hold of this and threw it straight at Pinocchio's head with all his strength. Once again Pinocchio ducked in time, and the book hit one of the other boys right between the eyes.

The boy who had been hit sank to the ground and lay very still. Everyone stopped fighting and there was a sudden silence. Then, thinking that the boy was dead, the others turned and ran off as fast as they could. Pinocchio was the only one who stayed, although he too was very frightened. He quickly ran and soaked his handkerchief in the sea. Placing this on the boy's forehead, he said: "Oh Eugene, please open your eyes. Answer me, Eugene. I didn't do it, believe me. It wasn't me. Look at me, Eugene. What can I do now? If only I had gone to school! Why did I listen to those fools? Mother warned me often enough, but I am always obstinate and go my own way. Even though it never does me any good. Whatever can I do now?"

It was all too much for Pinocchio, and he broke down and cried. Suddenly he heard the sound of footsteps and, looking up, saw two soldiers standing over him.

"What are you doing there on the ground?" asked one of the soldiers. "And what happened to this other boy? I can see he has been hurt on the head."

"I . . . I didn't do it," stammered Pinocchio.

"Then who did?"

"Not me," said Pinocchio.

"And what was it that hit him on the head?"

"It was this," said Pinocchio, picking up the book and showing it to the soldiers.

"And whose book is it?" asked one of them.

"It belongs to me," said Pinocchio quietly.

"Then you had better come along with us!" said the soldier. Before leaving, the soldiers called some fishermen and told them to look after the injured boy until next day, when they would come back. Then, holding Pinocchio firmly by the arms, they marched him off between them.

Poor Pinocchio hardly knew what was happening. He hoped he might be dreaming, yet knew in his heart that he was not. To make matters worse, he knew he would have to pass the fairy's house, dragged shamefully along between two soldiers. He would rather have died.

When they reached the outskirts of the village, a sudden gust of wind blew Pinocchio's cap off and he asked if he could pick it up.

"Go then, but be quick about it!" one of the soldiers said. Pinocchio slipped from their grasp and ran to fetch the cap but instead of putting it back on his head, he seized it in his mouth and ran off as fast as he could in the direction of the seashore. The soldiers started to follow but, seeing that he was too quick for them, ran instead to find the fastest dog in the village to chase him.

Pinocchio ran fast but the dog ran even faster and was soon gaining ground with every step. Before long both Pinocchio and the dog had disappeared from sight in a cloud of dust.

The green fisherman

The race went on and Pinocchio began to think that all was lost. The dog was right behind him and getting closer all the time, snarling and snapping almost at his heels. But the sea was getting closer too. When he arrived at the edge of the cliff Pinocchio just kept on running and made a magnificent jump into the sea. The dog tried to stop himself but he saw the danger too late and fell clumsily off the edge.

Pinocchio swam off without difficulty; the dog was not so fortunate. He was not a strong swimmer and the sea was too rough for him. The more he struggled, the further he sank under the waves. When he came to the surface again, he barked out, "Help, I am drowning, help me please!" Pinocchio was glad to be safe himself and at first paid no attention to the dog's cries, but as the dog continued to struggle and bark, Pinocchio began to feel sorry for him and at last he said, "If I save you, do you promise to leave me alone?"

The dog promised at once. Pinocchio still hesitated but, remembering his father's words that a good deed is never wasted, he took hold of the dog by the scruff of his neck and helped him to the safety of the shore. The dog had swallowed a lot of sea water and lay panting weakly on the sand but Pinocchio still felt safer at a distance, so he jumped back into the water and swam away.

"Goodbye, Pinocchio," the dog shouted after him. "Thank you for saving poor Alidoro. One good turn deserves another, and I shall never forget this. Perhaps one day I shall have a chance to repay your kindness!"

Pinocchio swam on, keeping close to the shore. After a while he spotted a cave amongst the rocks, with a cloud of smoke coming from it. Realizing that there must be a fire in the cave, he decided to go there to dry his clothes and warm himself up. As he approached the rocks, however, he felt something coming up under the water and carrying him up into the air. To his horror Pinocchio found himself trapped in a huge net together with lots of fish of different shapes and sizes, all wriggling and struggling.

The fisherman who was pulling in the net appeared at the mouth of the cave. He was as ugly as a sea monster, with grass on his head instead of hair, green skin, green eyes and a long green beard. When he had pulled the net out of the water, he carried it into the cave, which was dark and smoky. "Another good catch today," the green fisherman muttered to himself. "Now I can have a nice plate of fried fish!"

"Thank goodness I'm not a fish," thought Pinocchio.

There was a fire in the middle of the cave and on it was a large frying-pan. The fisherman plunged his enormous green hand into the net and pulled out a handful of mackerel. "Ah these mackerel look good!" he said, throwing them straight into the frying-pan. Then he pulled out a handful of sardines, and they went into the pan too. This went on until all the smaller fish had gone and Pinocchio was left in the net with a selection of big-eyed, many-coloured fish. In came the big green hand, grabbed him, took him out and held him up.

"What kind of fish is this?" said the fisherman, looking closely at Pinocchio and turning him over. "Perhaps it's some kind of crab!"

"Crab indeed!" cried Pinocchio. "May I inform you that I am a puppet."

"Puppet?" said the fisherman, looking puzzled. "Well that's a new fish on me. Still, never mind, I'm sure you'll taste good."

"But you don't understand!" said Pinocchio. "I'm not a fish at all!"

"You certainly talk well," replied the fisherman, "and for that I will offer you the choice of how you would like to be cooked."

"Given the choice, I'd rather not be cooked at all, but allowed to go home," said Pinocchio.

"You must be joking!" laughed the fisherman. "It's not every day that a puppet fish is caught in these waters. Do you imagine that I would give up the opportunity of tasting such a rare fish? I tell you what, I'll fry you with the other fish so that you have company."

Hearing this, Pinocchio began to cry and scream and struggle. "If only I had gone to school this morning," he sobbed. But it was no use. The fisherman took a strip of seaweed and tied Pinocchio's hands and feet to stop him struggling. Then he fetched a wooden bowl full of flour and plunged Pinocchio into it five or six times so that he was white from head to toe. Being so close to death, the puppet started to tremble and tried to beg again but, though he opened his mouth, no words came out, just a long groaning sound. Then he tried to beg with his eyes, but this did not seem to affect the fisherman at all: he just shook a bit of flour off, and carried Pinocchio over to the frying-pan.

Just as he was about to throw Pinocchio into the pan, a large dog ran into the cave, attracted by the delicious smell of the frying fish.

"Get out!" shouted the fisherman, still holding Pinocchio in his hand. But the dog whined and wagged his tail as if determined not to leave until he got something to eat. The fisherman shouted at him again and went to give him a kick, but at this the dog growled and showed his sharp teeth. At that moment a feeble little voice was heard in the cave: "Save me, Alidoro!" it said. "Otherwise I shall be fried and eaten!"

The dog recognized Pinocchio's voice at once, although he was surprised to see that it was coming from the white bundle which the fisherman was holding in his hand. Alidoro jumped at the fisherman, grabbed Pinocchio in his mouth and ran out of the cave as fast as he could. The green fisherman ran out after him, but Alidoro was too fast and the fisherman soon gave up the chase and returned to his more usual fishy dinner.

When they reached the path that led to the village, Alidoro put Pinocchio gently down on the ground. "I have so much to thank you for," said Pinocchio. "If you had arrived a moment later I would have been finished."

"It was just lucky I smelt the fried fish," replied the dog. "But there is no need to thank me. You saved my life first, and we must all help each other in this world. But as you say, a moment later and . . . "

"Don't talk about it!" Pinocchio interrupted. "It makes me shudder just to think of it!"

The two friends then said goodbye to each other and Alidoro went off home. Pinocchio saw a cottage not far off and went over to find a little old man warming himself in the sun.

"Excuse me," Pinocchio said to the man, "do you happen to know anything about a boy called Eugene who was hit on the head? I am so afraid that he might be dead."

"No, he is alive," replied the old man, "and has gone home."

"Then the wound was not serious?" asked the puppet.

"It might have been very serious!" said the man. "Apparently one of his schoolfriends, a good-for-nothing called Pinocchio, threw a

very heavy book at him and hit his head."

"Good-for-nothing!" cried Pinocchio. "What lies!"

"Why, do you know this Pinocchio?" asked the man.

"Only by sight," replied the puppet. "But he seems to me to be a very good boy, hard-working and always obedient to his father and mother."

While Pinocchio was talking in his most convincing voice, he happened to touch his nose and noticed that it had grown quite considerably. Suddenly he shouted: "Don't believe what I just said! I know Pinocchio very well and I must tell you that he is actually a very bad boy, lazy, disobedient, and always running off from school to get up to some mischief with his friends." As soon as he had finished speaking, his nose returned to its normal size.

Pinocchio then told the man how he came to be covered in flour and asked if he could borrow some clothes until his own were clean again. All the old man had was an old sack, so Pinocchio cut a hole at the end and one at each side and used it as a shirt. Then he bundled his own floury clothes up neatly, thanked the old man and set off for the village. He was in no real hurry. In fact the nearer he came, the more his feet dragged along. "What will mother fairy say this time?" he wondered. "Surely she won't forgive me again, and it serves me right! I never seem to change my ways!"

It was night-time when he eventually reached the village. A storm had come up and, as it was pouring with rain, Pinocchio went straight to the fairy's house. When he got there his courage deserted him and he ran away again without even knocking at the door. This happened three times, until at last he did give a little knock. He waited and waited. Half an hour later an upstairs window opened and a snail with a lighted candle on her head looked out.

"What do you want at this hour?" asked the snail.

"Is the fairy at home? It is I, Pinocchio."

"The fairy is asleep and must not be disturbed. And who is this Pinocchio, anyway?"

"The puppet who lives here. Please let me in quickly, I'm freezing!"

"All right, wait there," replied the snail. "I will come down and open the door, but I am a snail after all, and snails are never quick!"

An hour passed, then two, and still the door was not opened. Pinocchio was by now wet through as well as freezing, and at last he knocked again on the door. This time a window lower down opened and the same snail appeared. "I have been waiting for two hours!" said Pinocchio. "Could you please hurry up?"

"My boy," answered the snail, "I am a snail, and snails never hurry." And with that the window was shut again. Another two hours went by and finally Pinocchio lost all patience: he grabbed the door knocker in order to bang the door as hard as he could. Before he could knock, the iron knocker suddenly turned into an eel and, slipping out of his hand, jumped into the stream of water that was running down the middle of the street. "Well if that's the way it's going to be," shouted the puppet in a rage, "I shall just have to kick the door down!" And he kicked the door with all his might. He gave it such a strong kick that his foot went straight through the wooden door and got stuck. No amount of twisting and turning would loosen it and he had to spend the rest of the night with one foot on the ground and the other stuck through the door.

It was daybreak when the door finally opened: the snail had taken nine hours to get there. "What are you doing with your foot stuck in the door?" she asked, laughing.

"It was an accident," replied Pinocchio. "Could you please get my foot out for me?"

"You will need a carpenter for that, my boy," said the snail.

"Well could you at least bring me something to eat?" asked the puppet.

"Certainly," replied the snail. Three and a half hours later she came back with a silver tray on her head. On the tray was a loaf of bread, a roast chicken and four apricots. "The fairy has sent you this breakfast," said the snail.

Pinocchio was overjoyed at the sight of the food. When he began to eat, however, he found that the bread was made of plaster, the chicken was cardboard and the apricots stones. He felt like crying. In his despair he tried to throw away the tray, but instead he just fainted from exhaustion.

When he woke up, he found himself lying on a sofa with the fairy sitting next to him. He feared the worst, but the fairy said, "I will forgive you just once more, but woe betide you if you misbehave a third time!" Pinocchio promised that from that day on he would behave himself and work hard.

For the rest of that year Pinocchio kept his promise. He worked so hard that he came top in the school examinations and his general behaviour was so good that the fairy said to him, "You have been so good for such a long time that tomorrow your wish will be granted."

"What do you mean, mother?" asked Pinocchio.

"Tomorrow you will no longer be a puppet," she replied. "Tomorrow you will become a boy."

Pinocchio couldn't believe it. He was happier than he had ever been. The fairy said he could invite all his schoolfriends to a party next day, and there would be two hundred glasses of lemonade and four hundred jam doughnuts. The day promised to be a marvellous one, but . . . unfortunately in the lives of puppets there is always a "but" to spoil everything!

The Land of Fools

Pinocchio asked the fairy if he could take round the invitations to the party himself. The fairy gave permission, but said that he must be home before dark. "Oh I'll be back long before that," said Pinocchio. "I'll be home again in an hour."

"It's easy to promise," said the fairy, "but not so easy to keep one's word!"

"It is for me!" replied Pinocchio. "I'm not like the other boys. When I say I'll do something, I do it!" With that Pinocchio left the house, singing to himself. In less than an hour he had invited all his friends but one. They all said they would come, especially when they heard there was to be lemonade and jam doughnuts.

Unfortunately Pinocchio's best friend was out when he called. This was a boy called Carlo who was known by all the boys as Candlewick because he was as thin, straight and bright as the wick of a new candle. Candlewick was the laziest, naughtiest boy in school, but Pinocchio liked him more than all the others. He went back to Candlewick's house a second time, but Candlewick was still not there. After he had returned a third time without success, Pinocchio decided to go to look for his friend elsewhere.

He found Candlewick hiding in the porch of a farmer's cottage. When Pinocchio asked him what he was doing there, he replied, "I'm waiting for a coach to take me far away." Pinocchio then told him that he had been looking for him to invite him to the party, and that there was going to be lemonade and jam doughnuts.

"Sorry, I can't come," said Candlewick. "I am going to live in the best country in the world."

"And what's this country called?" asked the puppet.

"It's called the Land of Fools. Why don't you come too?"

"Me? No, I can't!"

"You should, you know, Pinocchio. It's the

most marvellous place. There is no school on Thursdays and Sundays, and the week is made up of six Thursdays and one Sunday! The holidays start on January the first and go on till December the thirty-first, and there are no teachers and no books. It's certainly the place for me, I can tell you."

"But what do you do all day?" asked Pinocchio.

"You play from morning till night. Then you go to bed. Then you get up and play from morning till night again. What do you think of that? Will you come with me? Yes or no?"

"Definitely not," replied Pinocchio firmly. "I promised my mother I'd be a good boy, and she wants me to be home before dark, so I'd better be off. Goodbye!"

"Just wait another two minutes," said Candlewick. "You might see the others. There are going to be more than a hundred of us."

"What if my mother tells me off?"

"Let her. When she's finished telling you off, she'll forget all about it. The coach will be here soon."

"No, no, I must go home." But still Pinocchio did not go. "Are you sure there are no schools there?" he asked.

"Positive. And no teachers and no books. Won't you come?"

"It's no good tempting me. I promised my mother that I'd keep my word. So goodbye, Candlewick. Have a good time, and think of me sometimes." Pinocchio turned to go, but after two steps he stopped again and asked, "Are you quite sure that the week is made up of six Thursdays and one Sunday? And that the holidays last all year?"

"Quite sure," replied Candlewick.

"What a delightful place," said Pinocchio quietly. "Still, I must be going. When will your coach be coming?"

"Soon. Why?"

"I'd just like to see the coach."

"But you'll be late. What about your mother?" asked Candlewick.

"I'm late already. When she's finished telling me off, she'll forget all about it."

Suddenly they both saw a small light moving in the distance and heard the faint sound of a trumpet. "Here comes the coach!" shouted Candlewick. "Now will you come, yes or no?"

"Is it really true that you never have school?" asked Pinocchio again.

"Absolutely never!" cried Candlewick.

"What a delightful place," said Pinocchio quietly. "Delightful, truly delightful."

The wheels of the coach were bound with rags and so it drove up in silence. It was pulled by twelve pairs of donkeys, harnessed together in double rows, four abreast.

The coachman was an extraordinary little man. He was extremely fat, with a small round face like an orange, a big mouth that was always laughing and a soft voice like a cat asking for a bowl of milk. All the children adored him and his coach was packed full of boys and girls, like sardines in a tin. They must have been very uncomfortable crowded together like that, but there was not a single complaint. They knew that in a few hours they would be in a country with no schools and that was all that mattered to them.

When the coach pulled up, the coachman said to Candlewick, "Tell me, my lad, are you waiting to go to the happy land? If so, I must warn you that there is not a single seat left."

"That doesn't matter," replied Candlewick

quickly. "I can sit on the roof." And with that he jumped up onto the roof of the coach and waited.

"And what about you, sonny?" the coachman asked Pinocchio.

"I'm staying here," replied the puppet firmly. "I'm going home to my mother and I'm going to school like a good boy."

"Oh come on, Pinocchio," cried Candlewick. "Come with us. We'll have such a good time!"

"Yes, come with us, we'll have such a good time!" shouted other voices from inside the coach.

"But I can't!" said Pinocchio again. "If I came with you, what would my mother say?"

"Don't think about that," replied Candlewick. "Just think that we're going to a country where we shall be able to run riot from morning till night!"

Pinocchio said nothing but just sighed. He sighed again. Then he sighed a third time, and at last he said, "Make room for me, I'm coming too!"

"There's no more room inside," said the coachman, "but to show you how welcome you are, you can have my seat up front. I'm happy to go on foot."

"No, I couldn't allow that," said Pinocchio.

"I know, I'll ride on one of the donkeys."

Pinocchio went up to one of the donkeys and was just about to get on his back when the donkey butted him in the stomach and knocked him to the ground. All the children in the coach laughed and cheered at this, but the coachman's smile disappeared. He went up to the donkey and, pretending to give him a stroke, smacked him hard across the ear. Pinocchio picked himself up and jumped straight on the donkey's back and all the children cheered and clapped their hands. Again the donkey kicked with its hind legs and threw Pinocchio back to the ground. Again there was laughter, but the coachman, instead of laughing, went to stroke the donkey again and smacked his ear even harder.

"You can get on now," the coachman said to Pinocchio. "That donkey is a bit obstinate, but my gentle stroking will have helped!"

Pinocchio climbed back onto the donkey's back and the coach started. A few minutes later, as the coach was rattling over the stones, Pinocchio thought he heard a soft voice saying to him, "Poor fool! You must always have your own way, but you will regret it this time!" Pinocchio looked all round, but he could not see anyone. The coach rattled on, the children inside all fell asleep and the coachman sang quietly to himself. When they had gone a few miles more, Pinocchio heard the same voice again: "Remember, little fool! Children who won't work and who don't like school, books and teachers come to a bad end . . . I know this from my own experience, and I'm telling you the truth. There will come a day when you will cry just as I am crying now, but by then it will be too late!"

The soft voice really frightened Pinocchio and he jumped down from his donkey to see where it was coming from. Then he saw that his donkey was crying, and that it sounded just like a little boy. Pinocchio told the coachman, and the little man replied, "Let him cry. He will laugh when he gets home again."

"But have you taught him to talk?" asked the puppet.

"No," said the coachman, "but he lived with some trained dogs for three years and he learned to mumble a few words. Let's not waste any more time. Get back on—the night is cold and the road is long!"

Pinocchio did as the coachman said and next morning they arrived in the Land of Fools.

It really was the most amazing place. The streets were full of noise and laughter and there were children everywhere. Some were playing with hoops, some with balls and others with shuttlecocks. Some were riding bicycles, others toy horses. Some were playing hide-and-seek, others tag. Some were singing, some were walking on their hands and others were walking about dressed as soldiers commanding cardboard men. Some were clapping their hands and others were whistling or clucking like hens. There was so much noise that it was impossible to hear yourself think. The walls were covered with scrawled writing and bad spelling: "We luv toyes!", "Down wiv skools!" and "No mor numberwurk!"

Pinocchio, Candlewick and the other children left the coach at once and it was not long before they had said hello to everybody and joined in all the games. The hours, days and weeks flashed past without them even noticing.

"What a marvellous life!" said Pinocchio whenever he happened to meet Candlewick.

"See, I told you!" replied his friend. "And to think that you didn't want to come! To think that you were going back to school to waste your time learning things. Thanks to me you are free of all that. That's what friends are for!"

"You are right," said Pinocchio. "It's all thanks to you. And do you know what the teacher used to say to me? Keep away from that Candlewick, he's no good and will only get you into trouble!"

"Poor teacher!" said Candlewick. "I always knew he disliked me and said nasty things about me. But I forgive him!"

"You're too kind!" said Pinocchio, putting his arm round Candlewick's shoulders.

Life continued in this way for five months, with every day filled with games and fun and no thought for books or school. Then one fine morning Pinocchio woke up to a most unpleasant surprise.

Pinocchio's ears grow

Pinocchio's surprise was a most unusual one. When he woke up, he scratched his head and discovered to his astonishment that his ears had grown enormously long. Not only that: they felt hairy! Pinocchio rushed to the mirror and was amazed to see that he had grown a huge pair of donkey's ears. He was so horrified that he started to cry and bang his head against the wall, but the more he cried, the more his ears grew and the longer and hairier they became.

Hearing Pinocchio banging and crying, the squirrel who lived upstairs came to see what had happened. She gasped when she saw Pinocchio, and he quickly said, "I am ill, Miss Squirrel. I feel very strange. Do you think I've got a temperature?" The squirrel put her paw on Pinocchio's forehead, and replied, "I'm afraid you are suffering from a very serious fever."

"What sort of fever?" asked Pinocchio.

"Donkey fever," replied the squirrel. "And

that means that in two or three hours you will no longer be a puppet, or a boy . . . " The squirrel hesitated. " . . . But a real little donkey like the ones you see in the market."

"Oh no!" shouted Pinocchio, grabbing hold of his donkey ears and pulling them as if he thought they would come off.

"There is nothing you can do about it," said the squirrel calmly. "It is fate. All children who are lazy, who hate school and spend all their time amusing themselves eventually turn into little donkeys. So it's no good crying now. You should have done something about it earlier!"

"But it's not my fault," sobbed Pinocchio. "It was Candlewick. I wanted to go home and go to school, but he kept on about the Land of Fools and what a marvellous time we'd have, and how it would be such fun."

"And why did you listen to that silly boy?" asked the squirrel.

"Because I'm a puppet with no sense!" cried Pinocchio. "If I'd had any sense I would never have left my dear mother, and I would no longer be a puppet but a real little boy like the others. When I see that Candlewick, I'll tell him what I think of him!" And he turned to go. At the door he suddenly remembered his donkey's ears and thought how embarrassing it would be to be seen in the street. Finally he found a very large cap which he put on to cover his ears, and off he went.

He hurried to Candlewick's house. When he knocked at the door, a small voice said, "Who is it?"

"It's me! Open up!" shouted Pinocchio.

"Just wait a minute and I'll let you in," came the faint reply.

It was several minutes before the door finally opened and Pinocchio was allowed in. Imagine his surprise when he saw that Candlewick was wearing a large cap, too! He pretended not to notice this and asked, "How are you today, Candlewick?"

"Very well, thank you," replied Candlewick politely.

"Are you quite sure?" asked Pinocchio.

"Of course I'm sure!" snapped Candlewick, less politely.

"Then why are you wearing that cap to cover your ears?" the puppet asked.

"The doctor told me to because I've hurt my

knee. Anyway, why are you wearing that great big cap yourself?"

"The doctor said I should because I hurt my foot," replied Pinocchio quickly. "But tell me something, Candlewick. Have you ever had trouble with your ears?"

"Never!" said Candlewick. "Have you?"

"Never!" cried Pinocchio. "Only since this morning I've got a bit of an earache."

"Me too!" said Candlewick, as if surprised.

"Perhaps we're suffering from the same thing," said Pinocchio. "Will you do me a favour and let me see your ears?"

"Certainly," replied Candlewick. "But first let me see yours."

"No, I asked first," said the puppet.

"I don't care," said Candlewick. "You show yours first!"

"I tell you what," replied Pinocchio. "Why don't we take our caps off at exactly the same moment. Agreed?"

Candlewick agreed to this and Pinocchio slowly counted to three. At the word three, they both took off their caps. When they saw that they both had the same long, donkey's ears, there was a terrible silence. Then, instead of feeling sorry for each other, they both began to laugh and prick up their ridiculous ears, and dance about. Suddenly Candlewick stopped, stumbled and said to Pinocchio, "Help me, Pinocchio! Help!"

"What's the matter?" asked the puppet.

"I can't stand up straight any more!" said Candlewick.

"Neither can I!" cried Pinocchio, stumbling and starting to cry. Then they both began to run round the room on their hands and feet. As they ran, their hands and feet turned into hooves, their faces became longer and turned into muzzles and their backs became covered with a grey hairy coat speckled with black. The worst and most embarrassing moment was when they grew tails. By then they were both crying but as they wailed their voices changed and before long they were both braying loudly, "Hee-haw! Hee-haw!"

Just then there was a knock at the door, and a voice said: "Open up! It's the coachman! Open this door or you'll be in trouble!"

At the circus

After waiting for a few minutes for the door to be opened, the coachman burst it open with a hefty kick. He was not at all surprised to see the two donkeys, and said with his usual little laugh, "Well done, lads! I recognized your voices when I heard you braying. I've come to take you to market!"

The two little donkeys just stood there with big, sad, pleading eyes. The coachman stroked them both and then combed and groomed them till their coats shone. Then he put ropes round their necks and led them off to market to offer them for sale. There were plenty of people who wanted to buy them. Candlewick was bought by a farmer whose old donkey had just died. Pinocchio was sold to the owner of a circus company, who said he would teach him to jump and dance with all the other circus animals.

The coachman was pleased with his day's work and went off with his pockets full of money. Indeed, some said that he was a millionaire, having earned all his money from the sale of donkeys. As you will have realized, he spent his time travelling round in his coach collecting all the lazy children who did not like school. When the coach was full, he would take them all to the Land of Fools, knowing that after a while they would turn into donkeys from playing all day and never doing any work. Then he took them off to market and sold them. It was an easy way to make money for there were always children eager to run off to the Land of Fools. All the coachman had to do was wait.

Pinocchio had a very hard time. When his new master put him in his stable, he found that all he had to eat was straw. He tried a mouthful but very quickly spat it out again. Then his master gave him hay, but Pinocchio couldn't eat this either. His master was annoyed and cracked his whip across Pinocchio's legs. Pinocchio began to cry and brayed: "Hee-haw, I can't eat straw."

"Then eat hay!" snapped his master.

"Hee-haw, hay gives me stomach-ache!" said Pinocchio.

"What do you expect, fried chicken and strawberry cake?" asked his master crossly, whipping him again. Pinocchio decided that it was best to keep quiet. At last the stable door was shut and he was left alone. After a few hours he started to feel so terribly hungry that he tried the hay again. He chewed it, shut his eyes and forced himself to swallow it. "The hay is not too bad after all," he thought to himself. "But if only I had gone to school, I could be eating bread and sausages now! Still, I must be patient." Sighing, he lay down and went to sleep.

Next morning he looked in his manger for more hay, but as he had eaten it all the night before, there was nothing to eat but the straw. "Ugh!" he said to himself as he chewed. "I hope this will serve as a lesson to all other lazy children. All I can do is be patient!"

"Patient indeed!" shouted Pinocchio's master, who came into the stable at that moment. "Come on, get moving! I didn't buy you to eat hay all day long. Now you must learn to dance the waltz and stand on your hind legs to earn your food."

It took Pinocchio three months to learn all his tricks and during that time he suffered more whippings than he could count. At last the day came when his master thought he was ready to give his first public performance. Posters were put up everywhere. They showed a picture of Pinocchio, the performing donkey.

That evening the circus tent was packed full with people an hour before the performance was due to start. The benches in the front rows were full of children of all ages, eager to see the little donkey Pinocchio. When the first part of the performance was over, the circus owner appeared as the ringmaster, dressed in a black coat, white breeches and big leather boots. He made a deep bow to the audience and began a ridiculous speech: "My lords, ladies and gentlemen! Myself being a visitor to this city, I wish to allow myself the honour, not to say the pleasure, of presenting to such a distinguished audience a famous little donkey who has been fortunate enough to dance before His Majesty the Emperor and all the kings of Europe. So thanking you, I beg you to help and encourage us with your applause."

This led to a great deal of clapping and laughter, which became even greater when Pinocchio made his entrance. He had been specially groomed for the occasion. He wore a leather bridle with brass buckles and there were two flowers in his ears. His mane was curled and each curl was tied with a coloured ribbon. His tail was plaited, his girth was made of gold and silver. The ringmaster introduced Pinocchio with another ridiculous speech: "My

lords, ladies and gentlemen! I am not here to tell you lies about the difficulties of taming this wild animal who was found grazing in the tropical mountains. Please observe the wild rolling of his eyes. In order to accustom him to a domestic life, I was sometimes forced to use the convincing argument of the whip. Unfortunately, my goodness to him only increased his viciousness. However, I discovered a bone in his head that the Faculty of Medicine in Paris has confirmed to be a dance bone. With enormous patience I have taught him to dance, as well as to jump through hoops and perform many tricks. But judge for yourselves. I leave you to admire him!" Then the ringmaster made another deep bow and told Pinocchio to do the same.

Pinocchio obeyed, bending both his knees until they touched the ground. The ringmaster cracked his whip and shouted: "Walk!" and the little donkey got up and walked around the ring. Then the ringmaster ordered: "Trot!" and finally: "Gallop!" While Pinocchio was galloping at full speed, the ringmaster fired a pistol and the little donkey, pretending to be wounded, fell instantly to the ground. When he stood up again, the audience clapped and cheered. Pinocchio looked up and saw in the front of the audience a beautiful lady with a gold chain around her neck. On the chain hung a medallion and on the medallion there was a picture of a puppet.

"That's a picture of me!" thought Pinocchio, and realizing that the lady must be the fairy, his mother, he tried to cry: "Oh fairy, dear mother!" Instead of words, the only sound that came out was a long, loud "Hee-haw!" Everyone in the audience laughed, especially the children, but the ringmaster hit Pinocchio on the nose with the handle of his whip to teach him that it was not good manners to bray at the audience. Poor Pinocchio licked his nose to ease the pain and when he looked up again the fairy had gone and her seat was empty. Pinocchio's eyes filled with tears but nobody took any notice. It was time for him to jump through the hoop. He tried three times, but each time when he came to the hoop he ran under it instead of jumping through it. At the fourth attempt he forced himself to jump high in the air but unfortunately he caught one of his hind legs on the wood and fell in a heap on the other side. When he tried to stagger to his feet he found that one of his legs was useless and he was led off to the stable.

Next morning the vet came to see him and said that he would be lame for the rest of his life.

"A lame donkey is no use to me," grumbled the circus owner and he told the stable-boy to take Pinocchio to the market and sell him at once. At the market Pinocchio waited to see who his next master might be. "Perhaps it will be a nice kind person," he thought. "Someone who wants a well-behaved pet instead of a worker."

To his dismay a sinister-looking man made the first offer. He looked sneeringly at Pinocchio's lame leg and thin body with its ribs sticking out. "Don't think I am buying him as a worker," the man said. "I want to make a drum from his skin for our village band." Poor Pinocchio trembled.

The man led the little donkey straight to the seashore, tied a stone around his neck, roped his legs together and pushed him off a rock into the sea. Weighed down by the stone, Pinocchio went straight to the bottom while the man kept hold of the rope and lay down on the shore waiting for the little donkey to drown.

The giant dogfish

When half an hour had passed, the man thought that his donkey must certainly have drowned and he began to pull in the rope. As he pulled he was surprised to feel no heavy weight on the end. He continued pulling it in, however, until at last the surface broke and out of the water came . . . a live puppet! Seeing a puppet instead of a dead donkey, the man thought he must be dreaming and he just stood there with his mouth open. Then he asked the puppet in a quavering voice, "What happened to the little donkey?"

"I *am* the little donkey!" replied Pinocchio cheerfully.

"Then how did you become a wooden puppet?" asked the man.

"It must have been the effect of the sea water," laughed Pinocchio.

"You're making fun of me!" shouted the man. "Now tell me the real story or I'll be very angry!"

"All right," replied Pinocchio. "If you'll untie me, I'll tell you the true story." The man agreed and at once took the ropes from the puppet's legs and the stone from around his neck. Pinocchio began his story at once.

"A long time ago I used to be a puppet, just like I am now. In fact I was on the point of becoming a real boy. But then I ran away from home and one day woke up to find that I had donkey's ears. I was taken to market and bought by a circus owner, who tried to make me into a famous dancer. One night I had a bad fall and injured my leg, so I was sent again to be sold and it was you who bought me. Then you tied a stone round my neck and threw me into the sea to drown! But fortunately for me, you reckoned without the fairy!"

"Fairy? What fairy?" asked the man.

"My mother," replied Pinocchio. "She looks after me as all mothers look after their children, even when they are foolish enough to run away. When she saw that I was drowning, she sent a huge shoal of fish to save me. They thought I really was a dead donkey and started to eat me. Some ate my ears, some my coat, and one of them was even kind enough to eat my tail!"

"Ugh, I'll never eat fish again," the man said. "Imagine opening a fish and finding a donkey's tail inside!"

"I agree with you!" laughed the puppet. "Anyway, when the fish had finished eating the donkey, they eventually got down to the bone, or rather the wood. And when they found that they could not eat wood, they just swam off and left me, without even a word of thanks. And that's how it came about that you pulled

out a live puppet instead of a dead donkey."

"That's all very well," said the man. "But I paid good money for that donkey. I'll just take you back to the market and sell you for firewood!"

Pinocchio did not wait to see what the man would do next. He dived into the water and swam off as quickly as he could. He did not even look round until he was at a safe distance and the man was just a tiny dot on the seashore.

Pinocchio was glad to be free again and he dived and played in the water like a dolphin. After he had swum for several miles he saw a white rock sticking up out of the sea. On top of the rock was a beautiful goat with blue hair, bleating and nodding to him. The goat's hair was the same colour as the blue fairy's hair had been when he first met her as a beautiful girl and Pinocchio swam as fast as he could towards the white rock, thinking it might be a sign from his mother. As he drew closer, however, the head of a horrible sea monster rose up out of the water. Before Pinocchio had time to hide in the waves, the monster was rushing towards him with his mouth wide open, showing rows of enormous teeth.

Pinocchio realized that this must be the giant dogfish described a long time ago by the dolphin and he was terrified. He twisted and dodged in the water while the goat on the rock bleated: "Faster, Pinocchio, faster!" As he came near to the rock, the little goat stretched out her front legs to help him out of the water. But it was too late. The monster dogfish came up behind him and sucked Pinocchio into his mouth. He swallowed the puppet so fast that he was already unconscious when he reached the monster's stomach.

When he woke up, he could not think where he was at first. It was pitch dark and there was a strong, fishy smell. From time to time great gusts of wind blew in his face. Gradually Pinocchio remembered what had happened and realized that the gusts of wind must be the fish breathing. After a while Pinocchio started to cry. "Help! Help!" he sobbed. "Please save me somebody!"

"Who do you think could save you?" asked a strange squeaky voice. I am the only one alive here, and I'm just a poor tuna fish who was swallowed at the same time as you. What sort of fish are you?"

"I'm not a fish," replied Pinocchio. "I am a puppet. Now what can we do to escape?"

"Nothing," said the tuna fish. "All we can do is wait here until the dogfish digests us."

"Not me!" cried Pinocchio. "I'm going to escape! Is this dogfish very big?"

"Big?" squeaked the tuna fish. "He is the biggest fish in the sea!"

While they were talking, Pinocchio thought he saw a light in the distance. The tuna fish could see it too. "It's probably someone else waiting to be digested!" he said.

"Perhaps that someone could help us to escape," said Pinocchio, and he slowly made his way in the direction of the light.

"Goodbye, tuna fish," he said. "I wonder where we shall meet again?"

"Who knows?" came the squeaky reply. "It's best not even to think about it!"

Pinocchio slowly groped his way in the direction of the light. The further he went, the brighter the light became and at last he reached it. It came from a candle stuck in an empty bottle. The bottle was in the middle of a little table and sitting at the table was an old man eating fish.

When he saw who the old man was, Pinocchio was filled with such happiness that he did not know what to do with himself. He wanted to laugh, he wanted to cry, and at last he managed a shout of joy as he ran into the old man's arms. "Oh father! Dear father!" cried Pinocchio. "I have found you at last!"

"Are my eyes deceiving me?" said the old man. "Can that really be you, my dear little Pinocchio?"

"Yes, it's me!" cried the puppet. "And I shall never leave you again, never, never, never! Oh you will forgive me, won't you father? It's so good to see you, I should never have left home, and I have had such a terrible time!"

"And how did you come to be here?" asked Geppetto.

"That's a long story," replied Pinocchio. "It

was like this. The day you sold your coat to buy me an alphabet book, I ran off to see a puppet show and the puppet master wanted to put me on the fire, but then he gave me five gold sovereigns to bring to you and then I met the fox and the cat who took me to the Lobster Inn but then they left without paying and I met robbers and I ran away but then they caught me and tied me up and then . . . " Pinocchio paused to catch his breath. He was so excited that his words came tumbling out faster than ever.

"And then the beautiful girl with blue hair sent a carriage to fetch me and the doctors said 'If he is not dead then it is a sign that he is still alive', and then I just happened to tell a lie and my nose grew and grew so I went with the fox and the cat to bury my sovereigns and the parrot laughed and my money was gone, but the judge sent me to prison. Then they let me out and I just went to pick some grapes when I was caught in a trap and the farmer made me his watch-dog and then a snake was in the way but he died so I went back to the beautiful girl's house but she was dead and a pigeon carried me off to see you and we flew all night but when we got there you had gone out to sea in a little boat and I waved and shouted but it was no use."

"I saw you too," said Geppetto, "and I wanted to come back to the shore, but the sea was too rough. Then this horrible dogfish swallowed me as if I were a breadcrumb, and I've been here ever since."

"But where did you get the table from?" asked Pinocchio. "And the candle, and the matches to light it?"

"That's simple," replied Geppetto. "The same day that I was swallowed a big ship sank in the storm and the dogfish swam down to the bottom of the sea and ate the ship. He just swallowed it in one mouthful. The only thing he spat out was the main mast, because that stuck in his teeth.

"Fortunately for me the ship was carrying lots of tins of food, biscuits, bottles of wine and coffee, candles and boxes of matches. But now I've finished all my supplies. There's nothing left to eat and this is my last candle."

"And when it's finished?" asked Pinocchio.

"When it's finished, we'll be left sitting in the dark," said his father.

"Then there's no time to lose," cried the puppet. "We must escape! I've already thought about it and what we'll have to do is get out through the dogfish's mouth and swim to safety."

"It's no good," said Geppetto. "I'm too old and weak. You'd better go on your own."

"No, I'll never leave you now," Pinocchio said. "I can carry you on my back. Come on, we must go at once. I'll take the candle and lead the way. Just follow me and try not to be afraid."

They walked for a long time through the dogfish, and at last they arrived at his throat. Fortunately the dogfish always slept with his mouth open, and he was fast asleep now. Looking up, Pinocchio could see out of his enormous gaping mouth. He could see the sea and the sky above.

"This is our chance," he whispered to his father. "The dogfish is asleep, the sea is calm and it's as light as day. Come on!"

They climbed up through the monster's throat and Geppetto struggled onto Pinocchio's back and put his arms round his neck. Then Pinocchio threw himself out of the dogfish's mouth into the water and swam to the surface as quickly as he could.

Pinocchio's dream comes true

Pinocchio swam as fast as he could towards the distant shore. He knew that his father was not very strong and indeed, before long Geppetto was trembling violently.

"Hold on, father," cried Pinocchio. "In a few minutes we shall be safe on dry land."

In spite of his brave words, Pinocchio was only pretending that everything was all right. Really he was beginning to feel very tired and he could hardly carry on swimming. He gasped and panted for breath until finally he said in a weak voice, "I'm sorry, father, I can't go on."

Father and son were on the point of drowning when they both heard a squeaky voice from below them saying, "Who's that up there?"

"It's me and my poor father," gasped Pinocchio.

"It's you, Pinocchio!" squeaked the voice. "You remember me, the tuna fish who was trapped with you?"

"But how did you manage to escape?" asked Pinocchio.

"I followed you and got out exactly as you did. Now, come and jump on my back, both of you. You will be on shore in four minutes."

They both climbed onto the tuna's slippery back and, as he had promised, very soon reached the shore. Pinocchio helped his father off the tuna fish's back. Then he turned to the fish.

"My friend," he said. "You have saved my father's life. I don't know how to thank you. Come here and let me give you a kiss!"

The tuna fish put his head out of the water and Pinocchio knelt down and gave him a kiss. Then with a flick of his powerful tail, the fish plunged under the water and was gone. Pinocchio offered his arm to Geppetto. "Lean on my arm, father," he said. "There must be a house nearby where we can shelter and get something to eat." They had not gone very far when they met two beggars by the roadside. Pinocchio recognized them at once. It was the fox and the cat.

The cat had pretended to be blind for so long that now he really had gone blind, while the fox looked old and mangy, and was paralysed down one side. He didn't even have a tail left, because he had sold it to a pedlar for a few pennies.

"Oh Pinocchio!" cried the fox. "It's good to see you! Could you spare two sick people a bite to eat?"

"Bite to eat," repeated the cat.

"Get out of my sight, you crooks!" shouted Pinocchio. "You tricked me once, but I won't fall for it again! You deserve to have nothing. Stolen money never did anyone any good." With that Pinocchio and Geppetto went on their way. A little farther on they saw a cottage in the middle of the fields. They went over and knocked on the door.

"Who is there?" asked a faint voice.

"A poor father and his son looking for shelter," replied Pinocchio.

"Turn the key and the door will open," said the voice.

Inside, they looked everywhere but could see no-one.

"I'm up here!" said the faint voice, and high up on a beam they saw a cricket.

"Oh, it's the dear little talking cricket!" said Pinocchio.

"You may call me dear now," replied the cricket, "but not so long ago you threw a hammer at me!"

"I know," said Pinocchio. "You can throw a hammer at me if you like, but please help my poor father."

"I shall help you both," said the cricket. "I just wanted to show you that we should always help others. If we do, we can find help when we need it ourselves."

"You are right, cricket," said Pinocchio, "and I have learned my lesson. But tell me, who does this house belong to?"

"It belongs to the blue-haired goat, but she went away yesterday crying and bleating 'Poor

Pinocchio, I shall never see him again!'"

"Then it *was* the fairy!" said Pinocchio, starting to sob at the thought of the dear fairy whom he might never see again. After a while he dried his eyes and made a comfortable bed of straw for Geppetto. Then he asked the cricket, "Where can I get something to eat for my father?"

"There's a farmer a few fields away," replied the cricket. "He will give you some bread."

Pinocchio ran all the way and soon found the farmer. But it was not so easy to get bread. The farmer said that Pinocchio would have to pay for it, and when Pinocchio explained that he had no money, the farmer said, "I'll tell you what. If you pump water up from the well, you can have a loaf of bread. But you must fill a hundred buckets to earn it. I need the water for my vegetables."

Pinocchio agreed at once and went straight to work. He was tired out long before he had filled a hundred buckets, but he did not give up. At last he had finished and the farmer gave him a large loaf of fresh bread. As he was walking out through the farmyard, Pinocchio noticed that one of the stable doors was open. Inside he could just see a little donkey. He went over towards the stable and looked inside.

"I'm afraid he's finished, that donkey," said the farmer. "He's totally exhausted from all his hard work." Pinocchio bent down and looked at the donkey's face. He thought he recognized his old friend. "What's your name?" he asked kindly.

"Can . . . dle . . . wick," replied the donkey in a tired little voice. Pinocchio felt very sorry for him and turned away to rub the tears from his eyes. "He was once a friend of mine," he said sadly to the farmer.

The farmer looked at him in amazement, then laughed in a rather embarrassed way. Pinocchio knew that he would never understand, so mumbling a few encouraging words to the donkey, he walked sadly back to take the bread to his father.

For the next five months Pinocchio got up at five o'clock every morning to pump water from the well in return for food. That was not all; he also learned to make baskets which he sold at the local market. With this money he was able to look after his father and, since Geppetto was still too weak to walk very far, he even made him a wheelchair so that he could take him out on fine days for a breath of fresh air. "If only I was strong enough to do my carpentry again," said Geppetto.

"There's no need for you to worry," replied Pinocchio. "When you are well, then you can think of that. Until then, let me do the worrying for us both!"

Pinocchio worked so hard that he managed to save some money for clothes, and one day he said to his father, "I'm going to the market to buy myself a jacket, a cap and a pair of shoes. When I come back, you won't recognize me!" And off he went, skipping and whistling to himself.

On the way Pinocchio suddenly heard someone calling his name. Looking round he saw a large snail crawling out from a hedge. "Don't you remember me?" asked the snail. "I was the one who let you into the fairy's house, you remember, when you got your foot stuck in the door."

"Of course I remember," replied Pinocchio. "But tell me, snail, where is the good fairy? What is she doing? Has she forgiven me? Can I go to see her?"

In answer to all these questions the snail said calmly, "I am afraid the fairy is in hospital. She is seriously ill and cannot even afford a bite to eat."

"Poor fairy!" cried Pinocchio. "That's terrible. If only I could help. I would give her a fortune if I had it, but I only have forty pence. Here, take the money and go at once to the fairy. Be as quick as you can and come back again to this place in two days. Then I should be able to give you more money. Up to now I've worked to look after my father, but from now on I shall work even harder so that I can look after my dear mother too."

Hearing this, the snail set off at a much faster pace than usual, looking almost energetic as she slithered along.

That evening Pinocchio stayed up until midnight making extra baskets. When at last he was asleep in bed, he dreamed of the fairy. In

the dream she smiled at him, then kissed him and said, "Well done, Pinocchio! As you have been so good, I will forgive you for all the bad things you have done in the past. Children who look after their parents deserve love and thanks, even if they have sometimes been naughty. Try to behave like this in future and you will always be happy."

At that moment Pinocchio woke up. He rubbed his eyes sleepily. Morning had come so quickly! He was just about to get out of bed as usual when he realized to his astonishment that he was no longer a wooden puppet, but had become a real boy. He touched his arms and legs nervously. They felt warm and soft. He ran his fingers through real hair. He looked round and saw that he was in a pretty little room that he had never seen before. He found new clothes ready for him beside the bed, with a new cap and a pair of new leather boots.

When he was dressed, he put his hands in his pockets and pulled out a beautiful little wallet, on which were written the words: "The fairy with the blue hair returns the forty pence to her dear Pinocchio and thanks him for his kind heart." Pinocchio opened the wallet and inside, instead of forty copper pennies, there were forty shining gold sovereigns.

Then he went to look at himself in the mirror. He still could not quite believe it, but there he was, a smiling boy with brown hair and blue eyes, a real mouth and, best of all, a well-shaped *real* nose. Could he still be dreaming? He pinched himself and it hurt: it was real! Suddenly he thought of his father and wondered where he might be. He went into the next room and there was Geppetto, looking well and happy. His bald head was covered by a new wig and he was carving a beautiful picture frame.

"Oh father!" cried Pinocchio, throwing his arms round Geppetto. "Do you have any idea how all this has come about?"

"It's all your doing," replied Geppetto with a smile.

"My doing?" said Pinocchio. "What do you mean?"

"It's quite simple really," replied Geppetto. "When children who have behaved very badly turn over a new leaf and behave well, they bring happiness to themselves and their families."

"And where has the old wooden puppet gone?" asked Pinocchio.

"He's over there," said Geppetto, pointing to a puppet leaning against a chair with its head on one side, its arms dangling and its legs crooked and bent. Pinocchio looked at the puppet for a long time, and then he said quietly, "How ridiculous I was when I was a puppet! And how glad I am that I've become a real boy at last!"